SELECT

SELECT

CHRISTIE MATHESON

RANDOM HOUSE NEW YORK

Text copyright © 2023 by Christie Matheson
Jacket art copyright © 2023 by Brenna Vaughan

All rights reserved. Published in the United States by Random House Children's Books, a division of Penguin Random House LLC, New York.

Random House and the colophon are registered trademarks of Penguin Random House LLC.

Visit us on the Web! rhcbooks.com

Educators and librarians, for a variety of teaching tools,
visit us at RHTeachersLibrarians.com

Library of Congress Cataloging-in-Publication Data is available upon request.
ISBN 978-0-593-56723-4 (trade)—ISBN 978-0-593-56724-1 (lib. bdg.)—
ISBN 978-0-593-56725-8 (ebook)

The text of this book is set in 12.75-point Adobe Caslon Pro.
Interior design by Megan Shortt

Printed in the United States of America
10 9 8 7 6 5 4 3 2 1
First Edition

For my three athletes
and everyone who loves to play.
May you always find joy in the game
(race, match, meet, practice).

"MY COACH SAID I RUN LIKE A GIRL. I SAID
IF HE RAN A LITTLE FASTER, HE COULD, TOO."

—MIA HAMM

1

LET'S GO

I'M SITTING NEXT TO MY LITTLE SISTER ON the city bus, holding her hand in my right hand and tapping my left hand on the back of the seat in front of us, as if that will help the bus go faster. I lean into the aisle for the millionth time, trying to see if the light ahead of us has changed from red to green yet. We're getting close to our stop, but we've been sitting in traffic that's been painfully, *painfully* slow because of an event happening in Civic Center Plaza, and another one in Golden Gate Park. When traffic is bad, going from one side of San Francisco to the other can feel like it takes forever. Especially when you don't want to be late.

Belle, my seven-year-old sister, whispers, "Are we almost there?" and looks up at me with anxious brown eyes. She's swinging her feet impatiently; they don't even come close to reaching the floor of the bus. I squeeze her hand. She wants to get to the soccer field almost as badly as I do, even though I'm the one playing in a game. I've told her we're playing against the other first-place team in our league, a team from Earthquake F.C. Earthquake is one of the biggest soccer clubs in San Francisco. And this team is better than any team we've played yet this season. Whoever wins today ends the season in first place.

Our mom is in the seat behind us, looking at her phone. She's oblivious to how long this bus ride is taking, and the magnitude of the game.

Finally, the light changes. The bus goes another block, then eases to a stop. Our stop. Belle and I jump right up, ready to scramble off the bus as soon as the doors open. My mom is still transfixed by her phone.

"Mom," I say. "It's time." The last thing I need is for her to miss our stop.

"Oh!" she says, startled. "Already?" She slides her phone into her bag and stands up. She's wearing her version of a "sporty" outfit today, which means jeans and a sleeveless top, and platform sandals instead of high heels. We have pretty different taste in clothes. And footwear. "Great! That was fast."

My mom doesn't move quickly. Still, we all get off

the bus before the doors close. Now we need to hurry to make it to my soccer field in time for me to have a full warm-up with my team. But my mom isn't hurrying. She's not even moving. She's reaching into her bag, trying to find something.

"Let's go!" I say, ready to get to my field, and hoping my mom will pick up the pace. She doesn't.

"Let's *go!*" I plead again.

My mom pulls out a little mirror and a lipstick. "Hold on, Alexa," she says. She's the only one who calls me Alexa. To everyone else, I'm Alex.

"Mom," I say. "You've got to be kidding me."

My mom almost never comes to my soccer games. She usually has to work on Saturdays, and when she doesn't have to work, she wants to sleep. I get it. She works two different jobs and is a single mom of two kids. She's tired.

But she has the day off today, and she wants to come to the last game of my spring season. I think it's because her horoscope told her it was a good day to watch sports. Really. My mom is into horoscopes. She isn't into soccer.

I guess it's nice of her to come, but this is ridiculous. It took her forever to get ready before we left our apartment, and now she wants me to wait while she puts on makeup? Nope.

I grab my little sister's hand. "Come on, Belle," I say. "We can run and Mom can meet us at the field. Whenever she's done." I roll my eyes.

"Okay!" Belle says. We start jogging, and I look over my shoulder and call, "See you at the field, Mom."

My mom is squinting into her mirror and tilting her head. She doesn't look up. "Sure, sure," she says.

Belle and I don't look back again.

"Alex," Belle asks as we get closer to the field, "why did Mom stop to put on lipstick?"

"I have no idea," I say. "But, Belle? Just so you know, you don't need lipstick at a soccer game."

"I know," Belle says, giggling.

We pick up our pace and make it to the field *almost* on time.

My coach, Jayda, is already there. So are the rest of my teammates. "Hey, Alex. Hi, Belle!" Jayda calls to us. "We missed you on the team bus this morning."

We don't actually have a team bus. Everyone on my team goes to the recreation center in my neighborhood, and before games, our team usually meets at the rec center and takes the bus together to wherever we are playing. But my mom took so long getting ready that we would have made them all late. So I texted Jayda and told her I'd go separately, with my mom and Belle.

I see the other team at the far end of the field, standing in two perfectly straight lines, waiting for a turn to shoot. They are wearing full warm-up gear—identical jackets and soccer pants over their uniforms, and even matching cleats. They also have matching team backpacks, lined up in a row near the sideline.

My teammates, all wearing rec center T-shirts and mismatched shorts, are starting to play keep-away in groups of four. From a distance, maybe it doesn't look very orderly, but it's a great way to warm up. I look toward the other team again. My teammates are getting *a lot* more touches on the ball than they are.

I tell Belle to go "help" Jayda until our mom gets there. Belle loves coming to my games, and she knows Jayda really well. Since my mom usually isn't at the games, Jayda helps keep an eye on Belle, and Belle sits on the bench with us and keeps track of water bottles and soccer balls, stuff like that. I hear Jayda call to Belle, "You ready to be my assistant coach today?"

I smile at that and jump into a keep-away game.

"I'm glad you made it," says Kiyomi, one of my best friends on the team. "Did you check out their uniforms?" she asks, flicking her long black ponytail in the direction of the other team. "Most serious ones yet."

She's right, and we've seen some pretty fancy uniforms

already. For this season, my team was promoted to the "upper house" league of San Francisco youth soccer. It's the highest level of rec soccer in the city—beyond that, you have to move to a "competitive travel" league. Not that our games aren't competitive. But we don't have to go outside the city limits to get to any of our games, which makes things easier since my family doesn't have a car. Neither do the families of most of the kids on my team. Of course, I wouldn't mind playing in a competitive travel league. I'm just not sure how I'd get there.

Anyway, the uniforms don't worry me. My team was promoted to this league after last season because we won all of our games. By a lot. There's a rule in rec soccer that a team isn't supposed to go up by more than five goals on the other team. Last season we won every single game by five, and we could have won by more if it weren't for that rule. Usually we had to stop scoring by the beginning of the second half and basically play keep-away for the rest of the game.

So now we are playing in upper house, where some of the teams are part of big soccer clubs, hoping to get promoted to a travel league and qualify for postseason tournaments: State Cup, Regionals, Nationals. You can tell them by their fancy gear, the way they laugh at our T-shirts, and how angry they get when we beat them.

We are definitely playing one of those teams today. I hear one player say to another, "Are they wearing, like . . . *T-shirts*?" They both crack up.

I know they want to win. They think they have to win. They think they're *going* to win.

Which makes me want to win even more.

I hear the ref blow her whistle to signal that the starters should get into position on the field.

"Let's *go!*" I say to my teammates, just like I said to my mom earlier. But this time I'm not annoyed.

I'm excited.

2
ONE, TWO, THREE . . . REC!

OKAY, THERE IS ONE THING I'M NOT SUPER EX-cited about. Jayda just told me I have to start this game playing goalie. We don't have anyone on our team who wants to be a dedicated goalie, so Jayda says the only fair thing to do is rotate. Everyone takes a turn playing a half in goal and then doesn't have to play goalie again until everyone else has had a turn. I'm fine with taking my turn, obviously. It's just that I would way rather be playing on the field.

Especially against a team that expects to crush us.

The Earthquakes look super confident when they strut out onto the field, and they bounce with energy as they wait for the ref to start the game. I think my team notices, and I swear I see a few of our players take a step back, as if to give them more space. That isn't good. We shouldn't be backing off before the game even starts.

"Get ready!" I call from the goal. "On your toes." A few of my teammates start bouncing around, too, and step up again, ready to play.

But the Earthquakes come on strong and outplay us during the first half. Our strikers take some shots on goal, but the other team takes more. I block as many as I can—this is more action than I've ever had in goal.

Then they get one shot by me. And we're down 1–0.

My hands go to my head and I grit my teeth in frustration. I'm not the best goalie on our team, and I don't want to be in here right now. But other than making as many saves as possible, one thing I can do is watch the other team's players carefully from the goal. I pay attention and notice patterns, strengths, and weaknesses. Who can't shoot or dribble with her left foot. Who always tries to dribble down the whole field herself and who looks for a pass. Who's fast. Who's slower. How their goalie doesn't have a strong kick but still takes their team's goal kicks—and when she does, she always fakes to one side, then sends a pass in the other direction.

At halftime, they still have just one goal. But we

haven't scored at all. When we come together as a team, I notice a lot of heads down, shoulders slumped. Jayda notices it, too, and doesn't let it slide.

"Chins *up*, girls!" Jayda says. And it's hard not to stand up a little straighter when Jayda talks to us. She's tall, and she gives off a total warrior vibe. In a good way. "You are hanging in there against a *really* strong team. You are only down by one goal. And you know what? All season long, we've scored more goals in the second half than the first."

She's right. We are a second-half team.

Still, I don't like being down at halftime.

"The main thing that's going to help you win this game," Jayda continues, "is believing—*knowing*—that you can. You can make great passes. You can shoot. You can clear it out of our end. You can beat them to the ball. You *can*. Do you know that?"

We all nod.

"Do you know that?" she says again.

"Yes!" we all shout.

And when the ref blows the whistle to call us back onto the field for the second half, we walk out there just as confidently as the other team does. For this half, I'm not in goal anymore. I'm playing center midfield. From this position I can move up and play offense or drop back and play defense as needed.

From the first kickoff, I play *hard*. If you're ever losing a game, I think the best thing you can do is play as hard as you possibly can. It's not the time to get down on yourself or back off.

The other team isn't expecting us to come out with this much intensity. About two minutes into the half, they pass the ball backward over their own goal line. So we get a corner kick. I've spent a lot of time practicing my corner kicks. Because even if I dream about scoring after an amazing passing sequence or a speedy breakaway, the fact is that a lot of goals get scored from plays like corner kicks.

About two years ago, when I was ten, I learned how to bend a corner kick into the goal. You have to strike the ball with just enough spin that it curves toward the goal, but not so much that it goes out before it even reaches the goal. Any time we had a game or I could get to an actual field (not just the courtyard of the local rec center), I would practice as many corner kicks as I had time for. I missed hundreds. Thousands, probably. But finally I learned how to get the ball into the net from the corner.

That's what I try to do now. I take a deep breath, raise my arm to let my teammates know the kick is coming, and connect with the ball. I watch as it sails up and over several of their defenders, the goalie . . . and into the far top corner of the net.

And just like that, the game is tied, 1–1.

I hear Belle cheering like crazy from the bench, along with Jayda and my teammates.

A few minutes later, the other team has a goal kick. I'm ready. Sure enough, the goalie takes it. She fakes left, then passes right . . . but her pass never makes it to her teammate. I see it coming and sprint as hard as I can to get there first, pretty much stunning the goalie, and it's an easy score. Oh, that feels good.

Now we're up 2–1. Belle and my teammates cheer. I look over at my mom to see if she's cheering, too, but she's staring at her phone.

This is why I don't mind when my mom misses my soccer games. She means well, but she just doesn't care about soccer.

A one-goal lead after being down a goal is great, but it's not enough. Because all it would take is one lucky shot from them, and we'd be tied again. I can't let up. Five minutes after my second goal, I steal the ball from one of their players and send a pass through a gap in the defense. Kiyomi chases the ball right through the hole, dribbles twice, then shoots low and hard to the corner. 3–1. I run to Kiyomi to give her a high five after her great shot, but there's too much time left in the game to celebrate now.

We keep fighting. Earthquake hasn't exactly given up, either. They bring the ball dangerously close to our goal a few times but miss shots wide and over the top.

Then, with about two minutes to go in the game, I dribble around three of their players before passing it off to Paloma, one of my team's strikers. She controls it and fires it right past the goalie. 4–1.

When the ref blows her whistle to end the game, our team goes crazy celebrating. Triumph and relief explode in my chest. We just beat the best team in our league— a team that expected to beat us easily.

The girls on the other team look shocked, and I feel a little bad for them. It stinks to think you're going to win a game, only to lose by three goals. Especially when it's the last game of the season.

But mostly I feel happy for my team. We just finished an undefeated season in a new, harder league. We *won* that league.

We give a quick cheer for the other team. "Good game, Earthquake!" we all shout.

They don't cheer for us. And when we line up to high-five them, I hear one of the girls mutter, "This team is so . . . *scrappy.*" She says it as if it's an insult, but I only feel pride.

And I don't feel bad for them after that.

The parents from the other team have set up a full buffet of snacks for the players, who are now gathering around it and eating and complaining about the ref's calls.

Our team doesn't have any snacks, but that's okay; we aren't expecting any. Jayda calls us in for a team huddle. We crowd around her, talking and laughing, wiped out but very happy. We quiet down just enough to hear what she has to say.

"Amazing game, girls," she says, beaming. Like, practically glowing, she's so happy. "You kept playing hard, even when you were down against a tough team today. But that's no surprise," she says, "because you played hard against every team in every game this season. I can't wait to see what you'll do next season."

That's when it hits me. It's the end of the season, and I know I'll wake up tomorrow morning with a sad ache in my stomach. I always do, after a soccer season ends. Jayda runs soccer clinics at the rec center all summer, which is great, but it's not the same. I try to swallow that sadness and focus on what we just did.

"I can't wait for next season, too!" I say. Because it's true. I'm always happiest during soccer season. I can't explain exactly why, but on the field is the one place where everything just feels right. No matter what is happening in the rest of my life.

Jayda smiles. "Hands in, girls. Rec on three!"

And we all shout, "One, two, three . . . REC!" one last time.

I love our cheer. I love our old T-shirts. I love my teammates. I am already counting down the days until I can be back out on the field, playing games with my team.

But what I don't know yet is that come fall, I'm not going to be playing with my rec center team anymore.

3

SAN FRANCISCO SELECT

WHEN IT'S TIME TO LEAVE THE FIELD, I CAN feel tears stinging the backs of my eyes. And I know Jayda can tell. She knows how sad I get when a season ends. She's been coaching me since I was five—well, five and a half. She gives me a hug. "Can you guys ride back on the team bus with us?" she asks, smiling.

"I think so," I say to Jayda, blinking back the tears. I figure my mom doesn't need time to get ready for the ride home, so there's no reason we can't make it to the bus on time.

"Yes! Ride with us!" Kiyomi says, then whispers, "And can you come over later?"

"Yes!" I whisper back to Kiyomi. She was the first

person I ever had a playdate with, back during my first season of soccer. My mom doesn't love it when we have people at our apartment, but when Kiyomi invited me over that first time, I learned that I love going to friends' houses.

I spot my mom on the far sideline, where she was for most of the game. She's finally stopped looking at her phone, and she's talking to some man I don't know. He has dark, slicked-back hair and a beard. He's wearing soccer warm-up pants and a matching jacket that says **SAN FRANCISCO SELECT** on the back, even though he doesn't look like he could last five minutes actually *playing* soccer, and he's kind of leaning over my mom.

San Francisco Select is another one of the biggest San Francisco soccer clubs, even bigger than Earthquake F.C. I've never played against a San Francisco Select team, but they have a reputation for being intense—and sometimes playing dirty. Also for having even fancier uniforms and gear than the team we played today.

Why is my mom talking to someone from San Francisco Select?

"Hey, Belly Boo," I say to Belle, who is helping Jayda shove the last of our worn soccer balls into a big mesh bag. Our team doesn't have a big set of matching balls with logos; Jayda is just happy that we have enough for every player. "Let's go get Mom so we can ride on the team bus."

"Okay," she says, and grabs my hand. We jog over together to my mom and the San Francisco Select guy.

As we get closer, I catch a little of what he's saying. "...Stop wasting her time...rec center coach has no idea what she's doing...little rec league...elite player... Nationals...college scholarship..."

That's when my mom sees me. She has a huge smile on her face. The man she's talking to also turns toward me with a smile, but it's the kind of smile that doesn't get all the way to a person's eyes. To me, it doesn't look friendly. Actually, it looks...kind of angry.

But that doesn't make sense. Why would this person I don't even know be angry at me?

"Alexa," my mom says, speaking slowly and carefully. The way she does when someone she thinks is important is listening. "This is Coach Austin." And then she adds, as if she's telling me he's a movie star or something, "From *San Francisco Select*."

I stare at my mom. Even though I've heard of San Francisco Select, I know my mom hasn't. So I can't figure out why she cares.

"Just call me Coach," the man says.

"Okaaaay," I say. "Coach." I reach out to shake his hand. "I'm Alex."

My sixth-grade Spanish teacher, Señora Sabedra, taught us that we should shake hands when we are introduced to people, and repeat their names to help us remember. "A firm and confident handshake," she always said, and had us practice shaking hands firmly, but not *too* tightly. And she said we should always look people in the eye.

Coach looks confused when I hold out my hand, but he slowly reaches out to shake it. Except it isn't a real handshake. It's the kind I've sometimes noticed men giving women in movies. His wrist is limp and he kind of barely touches the tips of my fingers. Plus, his hands are clammy. I pull my hand away and wipe it on my shorts.

He doesn't look me in the eye.

"Mom," I say. "We have to go so we can ride on the team bus."

"*Alexa*," she says, shaking her head at me and smiling apologetically at Coach. "Please don't be rude. I'm talking to Coach Austin. We're not in a rush. And your team," she says, waving her hand dismissively, "can ride the bus back without you."

My heart sinks. I don't want to stand here talking to

the angry coach with the greasy hair. I want to ride with my team.

That's when Kiyomi calls to me. "You coming, Alex?"

"Hang on a sec!" I call, before turning back to my mom. "Mom," I say firmly, not caring that Coach is standing there with his arms crossed, tapping his foot and looking over his shoulder. "It's the last game of the season. I really want to ride with the team. Please?"

My mom looks between Coach and me. Her eyes are wide, like a deer in headlights. She doesn't say anything.

"Go ahead," Coach says to me, and I blink. I'm not sure why some guy I just met gets to give me permission to ride the bus with my own team, but okay. "I'll see you soon."

Huh? Why is he going to see me soon?

Then he turns to my mom. "I have your number. I'll call you later and we'll get this all set up."

My mom smiles widely and says, "Oh, *thank you*, Coach Austin."

Seriously, what is going on? I want to ask her what's happening, but I don't want to keep my team waiting. "Let's go, Mom," I say, and practically drag her away from Coach. We meet back with my team and help them pick up a few last water bottles and sweatshirts. Then we head out toward the bus stop.

Coach has moved to a different part of the field complex, and we have to walk past him to get to the bus stop. As we do, I notice something weird.

Coach is introducing himself to a boy around my age who had been playing on the field next to mine. That isn't the weird part. The weird part is that when he meets the boy, unlike when he met me, Coach reaches out to shake his hand. Firmly. A real handshake.

And he looks the boy straight in the eye.

4

HE TOLD ME

THE WHOLE WAY HOME FROM THE GAME against the Earthquakes, my mom stares at her phone. She doesn't talk to me, or to any of the players or parents, or to Jayda. But as soon as we get off the bus and away from my team, my mom starts gushing about Coach. "He's just so smart," she said. "And he knows so much about soccer. Much more than your coach—what is her name again?"

"Mom," I say, annoyed. "You know her name is Jayda. And what makes you say he knows so much more than she does?"

I happen to think Jayda is the best coach of all time. And I happen to *know* my mom is clueless about soccer.

"Oh, just . . . he's . . ." My mom is still clutching her phone in one hand, but she waves her other hand around in the air, as if that explains things. I have no idea what she means. "And she's . . ." Here my mom waves her hand in a different way. I still don't know what she means.

"Alexa, I want what's best for *you*. Coach Austin's team is *the best*. He told me. If you play for the team he wants you to join, you will probably make it to Nationals. And if you do that, you can get a college scholarship to play soccer."

I have to admit that I'm paying attention now. I am aware that kids play for teams that go to Nationals, and that players sometimes get soccer scholarships. I just didn't know how to make it happen for myself. And I suddenly wonder if this team might help.

"And," my mom says, "he's going to let you play for Select for free. This might be the best thing that's ever happened to you. You'll never go anywhere if you keep going in this . . . this . . . What is it you play in now?"

"Rec league, you mean?"

"That's it. You need to be playing in, um . . ."

"Competitive travel?"

"Yes. With Select," my mom says, satisfied. She actually tosses her hair a little bit. Her hair is naturally brown, like mine and Belle's, but she likes to dye it bright blond. You can see a whole lot of the dark brown at the roots, though.

My mom's opinion about anything soccer related doesn't usually mean much to me. But some of the things she said are making me stop and think.

I'm only twelve, but I know that I want to go to college. And I know that there's no way my family can pay for it. But playing soccer could be a way for me to go to college for free. If I make it to Nationals, that has to help, right?

But I can't imagine leaving my team and playing for that Coach guy. The thought of it makes me feel squirmy.

"This all sounds great, Mom," I say. "But I don't want to leave my team. And playing for Select . . . I don't know. The coach doesn't have the best vibe."

"Oh, Alexa," she says. "You met him for about thirty seconds. I think his vibe is okay. Now, I don't know much about soccer—"

I stifle a laugh. That is the understatement of the year.

"—but I do care about you," she says, "and I think this could be the best thing for you."

I know she cares about me. And I am intrigued by the idea of playing for a team that could help me go to college one day. But *I* don't know if this is the best thing for me or not.

Maybe my mom's right, though. I'm already starting to feel excited about the idea of playing college soccer. And if that's ever going to happen . . . yeah. This might be something I can't risk passing up. Who knows if I'll ever get another chance like this?

So when Coach calls that night, my mom and I decide to sign me up for Select. My mom fills out all the forms on her phone. Which means that later, when I start having second thoughts around bedtime, she says there's no getting out of it for the next year.

It's a done deal.

She tells me I'll be playing for Select's best thirteen-and-under girls' team, called Superior. San Francisco Select Superior. "Isn't that a great name?" she says.

I stare at her and shake my head. "No," I say. "No, it's not."

It sounds way too show-offish to me. Not surprising, I guess, given that the club's tagline is "The best of the best." (My mom also loves that.) I've heard that before games, all Select teams have to do a really obnoxious cheer. It starts like this: "Don't mess with the best, 'cause the best don't mess."

Ugh. It hits me that I'm going to have to do that cheer. And tell people that my team name is San Francisco Select Superior. And have the greasy guy as my coach.

Suddenly, for the first time ever at the end of a soccer season, I'm *not* excited for the next season to begin.

5

FIVE AND A HALF

EVEN WHEN I WAS LITTLE, I COULDN'T WAIT TO start playing soccer.

Could. Not. Wait.

When I joined my first team, I wasn't even supposed to be playing. I was only five (and a half, as I would tell anyone who asked), and I wasn't technically allowed to go to the recreation center in my neighborhood, or be part of their soccer team, until I was six.

But whenever my mom and I walked by the rec center with Belle, who was a baby at the time, I could see through the fence to the small courtyard where the soccer teams practiced. When they were there, I would stop and stare. The rec center was crammed in the middle of a crowded block in a noisy neighborhood near downtown San Francisco, and there wasn't much space for soccer—but the kids who were playing didn't seem to care. I certainly didn't care. I just saw that they were running and dribbling and kicking balls and talking and laughing.

My mom got annoyed pretty quickly whenever I stopped to watch, especially if Belle was getting fussy. "Alexa, *why* are you interested in this?" she would say. "You don't even play soccer."

I begged my mom to ask someone from the rec center if I could play, and finally she did. We went inside to the front desk and she said, "My daughter sees your soccer team practicing when we walk by, and she wants to play. But is she even old enough?"

The woman working at the desk smiled down at me. She was Black, and she had her hair pulled back into a ponytail and secured with a stretchy pink headband, and her smile was the biggest and kindest I'd ever seen. I felt a pang of something, almost as if I knew her. I wanted to know her. "You want to play soccer, huh? I get it. I'm a soccer player, too." Then she turned to my mom. "You live in the neighborhood?" My mom nodded.

She looked at me. "What's your name?" she asked.

"Alex," I said, quietly.

"Her full name is Alexa," my mom said, "but lately she

wants us to call her Alex." My mom sighed and shook her head.

"Hi, Alex!" the woman said. "I'm Jayda. I love the name Alex. Like Alex Morgan!" She sounded excited.

"Who?" I asked.

"Who?" my mom asked.

"Ah! Alex Morgan is one of the best soccer players in the world," Jayda explained.

I grinned.

My mom looked confused again.

"Do you . . . do you *want* to have the same name as him?" my mom asked me.

Jayda laughed, but in a nice way. "Alex Morgan is a woman, and she's on the US Women's National Team." Then she looked at me again. "Are you six?" she asked.

I shook my head slowly, then looked down at my toes. I knew she was going to tell me I wasn't old enough to play.

"When do you turn six?"

My heart plummeted, because I wouldn't be six any time soon. It was only the end of August. "February twenty-second," I whispered, still looking down.

"Hey, you just turned five and a half," Jayda said. I smiled a little at that, and I nodded.

"Well," Jayda said, "usually we don't have kids come

here and play with our teams until they are six." I felt a disappointed ache in my belly, but to my surprise, Jayda smiled at me. And then she said the best thing I'd ever heard.

"But I coach our microsoccer team. Microsoccer is a league for the youngest kids playing recreational soccer," she explained to my mom, "and the league lets you play if you're five."

She turned to me. "So, I think we can make an exception to the rec center rules here. Would you like to play with us?"

I thought my heart might explode with happiness. I nodded. "Yes!" I said. "Yes!"

Even though my mom didn't fully understand why I wanted to play, she said I could. I went to my first practice a few days later.

And in the seven years since, I've looked forward to every game and every practice and every time I've even just gone to the rec center to kick the ball around with my little sister.

6

NOT ALL BAD

THE NEXT MORNING, MY MOM IS RUSHING around, trying to get out the door so she can be at work on time. She's working the opening shift at a department store today, as she does most days. I'll take my sister to her school and then get myself to my school, as I do every day. But then I start wondering how next soccer season is going to work, playing for a new team.

Up till now, all my practices have been at the rec center, which is close to our apartment. And Belle can go to the rec center with me. So what happens when I have practice somewhere else?

"Where does Select practice?" I ask my mom.

"Oh . . . ah . . . practice . . . um . . . it's . . . ," my mom says, distracted, as she opens and closes drawers in her room with one hand, while attempting to apply eye shadow with the other. "Coach Austin told me, and I'm trying to remember. It's . . . it's . . ." She trails off without coming up with anything.

"Really, Mom?" I say, frustrated. "I need to know. It kind of matters. What are you going to do with Belle while you're working, if I'm not here to help?"

My mom stops what she's doing and looks at me. "Alexa, I am trying to do a million things here," she says, frustration creeping into her voice, too. "The practices are . . . let's see . . . Beach something?"

"Beach Chalet?" I ask, feeling flickers of excitement and worry at the same time.

"Yes!" she says. "That's it. Beach Chalet. Do you know where that is?"

I do know where it is. I've had a few games at the Beach Chalet complex, and it's an amazing soccer facility, with a bunch of perfect turf fields. The rec center doesn't have a soccer field, so we practice on the flat cement area of the courtyard where I first saw the team, or inside in the rec center gym. I didn't even realize soccer was usually played on a field until I had my first game.

Still, practicing on an actual field will be amazing. The only problem is that Beach Chalet is *all* the way across the city.

"Mom," I say. "Yes, I know where it is. *Beach* Chalet? It's right near Ocean Beach."

"Oh," she says, wrinkling her nose, and I can tell she feels worried, too. Then she brightens up. "Well, you can take the bus to get there, and Belle can go to daycare after school."

Belle, overhearing this, shouts, "Noooooooooo! No!"

"Belle, what?" my mom says impatiently. "I don't have time for this right now."

"Mom, I don't want to go back to daycare," Belle says. I don't blame her. Our daycare is not a fun place. "It's all crying babies, and we have to be quiet when they're napping, and it smells bad, and there's nowhere to play outside, and they leave the TV on but with boring stuff!" Belle explains, the words coming out in a rush.

When we were little and our dad still lived with us, being at daycare was better than being at home in our tiny apartment, where it felt like someone (my dad) was always angry. He was usually mad at my mom, but sometimes he was mad at us, too. We had to be quiet and walk on eggshells when he was around. But he moved out after my first soccer season.

These days, Belle and I are happy when we're home together, or at the rec center. Which gives me an idea.

"Hey, Belly Boo. What if you go to the rec center instead? You can play on their microsoccer team."

Belle loves soccer, and it's about time for her to join a soccer team. But my mom hasn't let her start playing yet. Whenever Belle or I ask her, my mom says she has too much going on to handle another activity, but "maybe soon." Belle makes an excited squeaking noise, then looks at my mom hopefully.

My mom sighs, then smiles. "Fine," she says. "If that's *really* what you want. I guess it will make it easier for Alexa to join Select."

"Yes!" Belle shouts.

I grin. If my switching teams means Belle finally gets to play soccer, I guess it's not all bad.

7

SHE ALWAYS APOLOGIZED

AFTER I COMMIT TO PLAYING FOR SELECT, THE thing I dread most is telling Jayda. But I also want to talk to someone about it all, and Jayda is my go-to person for talking about anything to do with soccer. So I go to the rec center a few days later to find her, even though the first summer soccer clinic doesn't start till the next week.

She's sitting on the floor outside a storage closet, sorting through rec center T-shirts and folding the ones that are worth keeping. I feel an ache in my chest. I know I'm about to get a fancier uniform, but I love those T-shirts.

"Hey, Alex," she says when she sees me. "Aw, you look so sad. The next season will be here before we know it."

She's right. Jayda knows I always get this way once soccer's over. After my first soccer season ended, I woke up feeling like I had a knot in my stomach the next day. I didn't know how I was going to wait until spring.

Though, one thing happened that first winter that made things a little better. What happened is that my dad moved out of our apartment.

It shouldn't have been a surprise. He never really liked being there. When he wasn't working at his job at a gym somewhere downtown, he was usually out doing something else. We never knew exactly what, and we didn't meet any of his friends.

And when he *was* home, he slept a lot, or lay on the couch watching TV or playing video games. He yelled at my mom if we weren't quiet, and she always apologized and made us go into our little bedroom and close the door.

He also sometimes called my mom an idiot or stupid, and was mean to her if he thought she didn't look nice. She always apologized.

None of that ever felt right to me, even when I was five. I didn't know exactly why, or how to explain it at the time. Once I tried to talk to my mom about it.

"Why do you always say sorry," I asked, "when Dad is mean to you?"

Then she got mad and told me I just didn't understand

what it was like between grown-ups. And she told me not to say anything like that again. Especially not in front of my dad.

So I kept quiet after that. But when he moved out, I wasn't very sad.

Our mom was sad, though. I remember coming out of my room and finding her on the floor, curled up in a ball and crying.

I put my hand on her back and asked her if she was okay. "It will be better when he's not here," I said. "You won't have to say sorry so much."

She stopped crying for a second and thought about it.

"Maybe you're right," she finally said.

Jayda claps her hands, snapping me out of my thoughts. "Instead of being sad, let's get excited and work as hard as we can this summer to get ready for fall. Can you get excited with me?"

"No," I say dully, and then just blurt it out. "Because I can't play with you next season."

She looks up from the shirt she's examining.

"What?" she says. "What do you mean?"

"I'm going . . . ," I start to say, and my voice gets shaky. I swallow. "I'm going to play for a club team. Comp travel. My mom talked to the coach after our game, and he convinced her it's the best thing for me. And maybe . . . maybe it is, because I want to play in college one day. But I don't want to leave our team."

I brace myself, wondering if Jayda will get mad. But I should have known better. Jayda never gets mad, though she looks up at me with a concerned frown.

"Alex, I'm sure your mom really is trying to do what's best for you. She knows how much you love soccer. But . . . which club team?"

"San Francisco Select," I say.

Jayda nods once, as if my answer confirms what she was expecting. "Oh boy," she says. "Yeah, I saw Andy talking to your mom. I should have asked her about it."

"Who's Andy?" I ask.

"The founder of Select," Jayda explains. "The guy who was talking to your mom after our game against Earthquake."

"Oh. Coach Austin. Do you know him?" I ask.

"A little," she says.

"And?" I ask.

She pauses, and I can tell she's struggling to decide what to say.

"And . . . listen, Alex," she continues. "It's going to be okay. You're going to play a lot of soccer, against some great teams. It could be good for your game. But . . ." She trails off.

"But what?" I ask.

She looks me straight in the eye. "But no matter what happens, try not to get too caught up in it. Don't let him make you feel bad when you probably haven't done anything wrong."

That sounds too much like what my dad used to do to my mom. I wonder why a coach would ever do that to his players. There's no way I'll let that happen to me.

Then Jayda adds, "And don't forget how much you love soccer."

"I could never forget how much I love soccer," I say.

"Good," she says. "Now let's go play."

8

GREAT SHIRT

I GO TO THE REC CENTER TO PRACTICE WITH
Jayda almost every day that summer, and the time flies.
Suddenly fall practices are about to start.

Usually the first thing I think when I wake up in the
morning is, *Do I have soccer today?* And the same thought
runs through my head when I wake up on the morning
of my first Select practice. I know immediately the answer is yes, but I'm less excited about it than I usually am.
I already miss Jayda and the rec center.

When I picked up my gear at the Select office last
week, Coach told me it was mandatory to use my new
Select backpack for all practices and games. Last night, I
packed my new backpack with gear so I can take it with
me to school, because I'm going to have to leave straight

from school to go to practice. School gets out at three, and practice doesn't start until four-thirty, but I don't know how long it will take me to get there.

My Select practices are at the Beach Chalet soccer fields, which are at the western edge of Golden Gate Park, almost at the ocean. I know it *should* be a forty-minute ride on the 5 bus from my neighborhood to Fulton and Forty-Sixth, where I have to get off. But we'll be getting closer to rush hour, and I know how crowded and slow and unpredictable buses can be. Plus, I have to get from the bus stop to the field, and although they're pretty close to each other, I don't want to take any chances.

All day at school, I can't keep my feet still and I have trouble concentrating. I think I look at the clock every thirty seconds. Luckily it's only the second day of school, so most teachers are still learning our names—I don't think any of them know mine, yet—and going over the rules and telling us what we'll be doing this year. I hope I'll be able to focus better after I get my first practice out of the way. Last year I kept hearing about how hard seventh grade is compared to sixth. I got mostly As in sixth, and I want to get *all* As in seventh. It's going to be easier to get a college scholarship someday if my grades are good.

When the final bell rings at three, I jump out of my seat in math class and start running to my locker. Mr. Schaeffer, my English teacher, sees me and calls out, "Alex! Don't run in the halls, please."

Great. The one teacher who has learned my name wants to slow me down.

I dial it down to a speed walk. A few seconds later, a group of eighth-grade boys, all in football jerseys, sprint past me, going in the other direction. I look over my shoulder to see if Mr. Schaeffer is still out in the hall.

He is.

I watch to see if he says anything to the football boys about not running.

He doesn't.

If they are allowed to run, then I am, too. So I do.

At my locker, I grab my backpack and keep running, all the way out the front door of Eisenhower Middle School, and four blocks to the bus stop.

My bus stop is across the street from another bus stop, one for a bus going in the opposite direction. Only one person is waiting at that stop. I can tell from across the street that he's anxious for the bus to come. He's pacing and tapping his hand against his thigh, and he keeps looking in the direction that the bus will be coming from. He looks even more impatient than I feel.

As I wait for my bus, I wonder where he's going. His bus pulls up first and as it does, I see an older woman, her hands full of bulging shopping bags, moving as quickly as she can toward his bus stop. She's trying frantically to wave her hands and get the bus driver's attention, but that's hard to do when you're carrying a bunch of bags. And I don't know if there's any way I can help her from across a very busy street.

The woman trips over something on the sidewalk, stumbles, and drops one handful of bags. I'm glad she doesn't fall. She gathers up the bags she dropped and keeps going toward the bus stop.

The man waiting for the bus notices her, and I feel my shoulders relax. At least the man can ask the driver to wait. I've done that before, and drivers are usually happy to wait if they know someone is about to get on.

But then—the man must not have said anything. And the bus driver must not have seen her, because the bus slowly pulls away when the woman is about five feet from the bus door. She drops one armful of bags and reaches out with that hand, but the bus keeps moving. Her head bows forward and her whole body kind of slumps over.

Suddenly my head starts buzzing with anger at that man from the bus stop. I *know* he saw the woman. Would it have ruined his day that much to ask the driver to wait, and to have the bus leave the bus stop fifteen seconds later?

I think there are two kinds of people in the world—the people who would have asked the driver to wait, and the people who wouldn't. For some reason an image of Coach flashes through my head, and I consider which type he might be.

Just then my own bus pulls up. Before I get on, I look both ways to see if anyone is running to make it to this bus, but it's all clear.

I get on the bus and find a seat with an empty seat next to it. Whew. I have a plan for getting changed into my practice gear. It would have been easier to go home before practice, or at least get a ride, but since neither is an option for me, I need a different strategy. So I'm wearing my soccer shorts under a skirt, and a T-shirt that's easy to wiggle out of once I have a soccer shirt on over it. It's easier to do all of this with no one sitting next to me.

Next I pull off my school shoes and put on shin guards, socks, and cleats. I'm ready to go before the bus has traveled five blocks. With my gear on, I start to feel more of the excitement I'm used to. I'm ready to play.

Now I just have to sit here and stare out the window as the bus inches along in the afternoon traffic.

It's going to take a while.

As I sit on the bus, I start to feel like I'm forgetting something. It nags and scratches at my brain for a minute, before I realize that this is the exact moment when I would have been picking Belle up from school. It's the first afternoon since she started kindergarten last year that I haven't been the one to pick her up. Every day last year, I met her outside her school and we went to the rec center together.

My heart hurts a little when I think about that now.

I look at my phone to check the time. Yep, she's getting out right about now, at 3:20. Of course, she knows I won't be there. My mom can't be there, either, because she's working. So the plan is for Belle to ride a school bus that will drop her off at the rec center. And when she gets there, she has her very first soccer practice.

I can't believe I won't be at the rec center for that. Belle was so quiet last night while we were getting our backpacks ready for school. She never said it, but I think she was nervous about going to the rec center on her own. I tried to think of something to do for her to make it seem like I would be with her, in a way. So I gave her my old rec center T-shirt, the one that had been my uniform the first season. It had been way too big for me then, and it was too big for Belle now, but she still wore it to school today.

I'm almost positive Belle will get to the rec center with no problems, but I text Jayda just to make sure.

> Hi! Can you text me when
> Belle gets there?

She writes back immediately.

> For sure. Her first practice today!

Jayda is going to be Belle's coach, and hearing from her fills me with relief. I won't be there, but at least Jayda will be looking out for Belle. I write back quickly.

> Thanks! She's so excited.

A second later I text one more thing.

> I miss playing with you already.

Jayda sends a heart emoji. Then she adds:

> I miss you, too. But you are going
> to make the BEST of this season!

And then, a few minutes later, I hear from Jayda again.

> Belle's here! Wearing your old
> soccer shirt! 😊

I smile.

I remember how excited I was the first time I wore it. The morning of my first soccer game, I woke up while it was still dark because I was so excited, even though the game wasn't going to start for hours. I put on some shorts and my game shirt, a rec center T-shirt with the number 5 on the back. Jayda said I should have that number to celebrate being the youngest player on our team.

Last night I told Belle I'd wear a rec center soccer T-shirt to my practice today, too. So now we match, even though we aren't together. I have a Select practice jersey, but I figure it's fine to wear any shirt to practice. I could wear anything I wanted to my rec center practices.

Once I know Belle is safely at the rec center, I lean back against my seat, exhale, and feel my shoulders relax. I'm just going to soccer practice, after all. Sure, it's a new team for me, but Coach recruited me for the team. He wouldn't have done that unless he thinks I'm good. And no matter who I'm playing with, it's still soccer. Still my favorite thing to do in the whole world.

When my bus stops at Fulton and Forty-Sixth, I get off, tighten the straps of my backpack, and jog a block up Fulton toward the entrance to Golden Gate Park. As I'm jogging, I can see the ocean sparkling in the sunshine.

I stop for a second just to look. Our apartment is only a bus ride away from the ocean, but we almost never come out here. I decide to bring Belle with me sometime soon, so we can look at the water, and then go kick a ball around at my soccer field. She will love this.

I arrive at the Beach Chalet soccer fields about twenty minutes before practice is supposed to start. These fields are even nicer than I remembered. They're all bright green turf, and they look perfect on this sunny September day. There's no trash anywhere. The lines are perfect. There's a big parking lot and a little playground—another reason to bring Belle here—and there are trees all around.

This is going to be very different from practicing in the rec center courtyard.

There are a bunch of fields here, but I know I need to find pitch 1, field C. It takes me a few minutes to figure out exactly where that is. As I'm about to head over to it, a group of girls around my age—all wearing bright red Select practice jerseys and carrying backpacks like mine—jogs past me, toward the field where I'm going.

Okay. These must be some of my teammates. I turn back toward the parking lot to see if more are coming. There's a line of really nice, big cars moving slowly near the entrance to the field. They stop, and a few doors open. More girls wearing Select practice jerseys get out and run toward our field.

I look down at my own T-shirt and suddenly feel a prickle of panic go up my arms and legs. I shouldn't have worn some beat-up old shirt to Select soccer practice. Coach had made a big point about always using the Select backpack, but he hadn't said anything about mandatory practice gear. Now I don't have time to change or do anything other than run over to join my new team.

While wearing the wrong shirt.

I take a deep breath and jog to the spot where about twelve girls in Select jerseys are now putting down their backpacks—at least I have the right one of those—and pulling out soccer balls.

I notice something strange as I run up to them: no one is talking. At the beginning of practices with my rec center team, Jayda always had to quiet us down before she started talking to us. But all the girls from Select are silent.

Then Coach suddenly appears next to the group. I didn't see him coming and honestly don't know where he came from. All the girls stand up straight and put one foot on top of their ball. I do the same.

Coach glances at me. He gives me a funny look when he notices my T-shirt, but he doesn't say anything.

"We have a new player joining us today," Coach says. He points at me. "This is Alexa." The girls look at me. One or two of them smile. A couple of others raise their eyebrows at my shirt. I feel my cheeks get hot.

"Actually, it's Alex," I say quickly. If I don't correct it now, they might be calling me Alexa all season.

A few of the girls looked surprised when I spoke up. What's that all about?

But then Coach's eyes narrow, and anger flashes across his face. He opens his mouth as if he's about to say something to me. I feel my body tense, waiting for—I don't know what. But then he seems to stop himself.

I wonder what he was about to say. I wonder if that has anything to do with why the girls looked surprised when I corrected him—about my own name. I wonder if it's better to keep my mouth shut around him, no matter what he says. The idea of that makes me feel squirmy inside.

The other girls certainly seem to want to keep quiet. None of them introduce themselves to me. When someone joined our team at the rec center, Jayda always had us go around and say our names a few times so the new player could get to know us. She would also ask the new player a few fun questions about herself.

Coach just tells us what our first warm-up drill will be. I don't recognize the name of the drill, and he doesn't explain it. So I just follow along with what the other girls do—the girls whose names I don't know.

When Coach walks away from us to set up cones at the other end of the field, one of the girls stops near me and says, "Great shirt." I look up at her, surprised. She has long, shiny brown hair and of course she's wearing a Select shirt. Then I look down at my shirt and smile. Maybe it isn't a problem that I'm wearing this. Maybe it's actually a good thing, because it's obvious I'm not trying to show off.

"Thanks," I say. "It's from my old team," I add, feeling proud and a little sad as I say it.

"Uh, yeah. We know," she says, rolling her eyes. Then she smirks and dribbles away.

Oh.

She doesn't think it's a great shirt.

Got it.

That's the first time any player from Select speaks to me. No one else hears, or so I think.

But a moment later another girl, this one with blond hair and goalkeeper gear, dribbles past me. "Don't worry about Apple," she says, pausing for a moment.

Huh? What apple? I wonder.

"She's clueless," the girl continues, tucking a few flyaway pieces of her hair into a stretchy pink headband that looks a lot like the one I wear for games. Mine is made from pink athletic wrap, just like Alex Morgan's. "I'm Olivia, by the way," she adds. "But everyone calls me Liv." She dribbles off again.

I smile. Another team, another Olivia. There were two Olivias on my rec center team.

And Apple is the name of the girl who not-so-subtly made fun of my rec center shirt. She's a striker, like I am, and she was their leading scorer last season.

And apparently she is not happy about me joining the team.

The soccer part of practice is fine. I keep up with my teammates—more than keep up, actually—and by the end I'm pretty sure I'm going to be able to contribute a lot during games. But no one except Liv talks to me. To be fair, they don't talk much to each other, either.

Maybe I need to start talking to everyone. Next time.

Later, when I pick up Belle at the rec center, Jayda asks me how my first Select practice went.

"It was okay," I say.

"Just okay, huh? Practicing with the almighty Select isn't the best thing ever?" Jayda says, smiling.

"Not really," I admit. "They didn't like my shirt," I add.

"What?" Jayda asks with a laugh.

"My shirt. I'm pretty sure some of them were making fun of it, because it's old and not fancy like the Select shirts," I explain.

"Ah," Jayda says, nodding. "How did that make you feel?"

"Not great," I say.

"No. I'll bet it didn't," she says. "But I can tell you something. I know this won't help the way you feel right now, but believe me: the fact that they made fun of your shirt says way more about them than it does about you."

I shrug. She's probably right.

But that doesn't make it easier to be the one getting made fun of.

Jayda looks closely at me. "What else?" she asks.

I sigh. "I just . . . I get the feeling that Coach can be

kind of . . . mean. It seemed like he got mad at me just for speaking up and telling him what my name is."

Jayda sighs, too. "Yeah," she says. "I'm not surprised. But, Alex? Don't stop speaking up, okay?"

I nod, feeling a ripple of energy go through me. Because I know she's right.

9

WAIT. WHERE IS IT?

THERE'S A LONG LIST OF THINGS MY MOM AND I didn't realize about what it would be like playing for Select. One of the things is that the games would not all be in San Francisco, like they were with my rec center team. My Select team is a travel team, which means we have games all over the place, often way outside the city.

For the other girls on my team, this is no big deal. Wherever they need to go, their parents drive them. Or in some cases, their family's driver drives them. Before I joined Select, I didn't know people had drivers in real life.

My family doesn't even have a car.

I didn't think much about this, either, until we got our fall schedule. Our first game is an away game against

Burlingame United. In Burlingame. Which I have never heard of.

When Coach first mentions Burlingame at practice, I raise my hand.

"What, Alex?" he asks.

"I don't know that field," I say. "Burlingame Field. Where is it?"

He looks at me like I have a unicorn horn growing out of my head. "It's not a field," he says slowly. "It's a *town*."

"Okay," I say. "But wait. Where is it?"

"The Peninsula, Alex. Look it up."

So I do, when I get home. I learn that Burlingame is a very nice suburb, about twenty miles south of the city. I also learn that it can take a long time to go twenty miles on public transportation. One hour and twenty-seven minutes, to be exact. I'll have to walk to the Muni stop closest to our apartment, take the bus to the stop near the Caltrain Depot, then take the Caltrain 410 southbound to Burlingame, and then walk to the field. *If* I time it perfectly, and get on the right bus and train, *and* everything is running on schedule.

We have a game there at ten in the morning on Saturday, and we have to be at games an hour before kickoff.

So, to be safe, I have to leave our apartment by seven, or a quarter past seven at the latest.

There's no way my mom will go with me for this, no matter what her horoscope says.

So I'm going to have to do it alone.

I think about when I used to meet Jayda at the rec center and ride the bus with her to our games. And how that had seemed hard, and how I always used to wish I had a parent to go with me.

Now doing that seems easy.

And I'm starting to wish I could just go to my game with Jayda.

10

MOM'S NOT HERE

I SET MY ALARM FOR SIX A.M. ON THE DAY OF my first game, but I'm awake long before it goes off. It feels like I woke up every few minutes during the night. Each time I woke up, I worried about something. Sometimes I worried about being late to the game. Sometimes I worried about getting on the wrong bus or the wrong train. Sometimes I worried about not playing well enough, and my teammates getting mad at me. Sometimes I worried about playing *too* well, and my teammates getting mad at me.

And sometimes I just worried about being awake. Not getting enough sleep isn't good for soccer players.

But I am definitely already awake when I hear the

first beep from the alarm on my phone. I turn it off as quickly as I can, hoping Belle won't wake up.

She does anyway.

"You 'wake, Alex?" she mumbles. She is sleeping on her stomach, as usual, and her face is mostly smushed into her pillow.

"I'm awake," I whisper as I climb down from my top bunk. "Go back to sleep, okay?"

" 'Kay," she says. Then she sits up in bed.

"Is your game today?" she asks.

"Yep," I say.

"Can I come?" she asks.

"Not this time, Belly Boo," I say. Although I kind of wish she could, so I wouldn't have to get there and back all by myself. But I also don't want to drag her with me when I'm not exactly sure where I'm going, and when I'm worried I might get lost. "I have to go all the way to Burlingame, remember?"

"Oh. Yeah," she says. She's quiet for a moment, and then she says, "I wish I could go."

Another thing my mom and I didn't think about was how much extra time Select would take. More practices. More games. Games farther away. More tournaments. All of which means less time I can spend with Belle. And it isn't like my mom has tons of time to spend with her when I'm not around.

"So do I. Next time," I say. "Promise."

I cringe when I hear myself say that, even though I mean it.

Because I sound like our mom, lately.

"Promise!" she'll say, whenever she tells us we'll get to do something another time. She might think she means it at the time, but she never follows through anymore. And lately she has been saying it more and more, especially since she met Xander.

Xander is her boyfriend. She went out with him maybe twice before he came over to meet Belle and me. He isn't very interested in us. But he is interested in having my mom do exactly what he wants her to do, anytime he wants her to do it. The way she is with Xander kind of reminds me of how she was with my dad. But Xander isn't our dad. And I hate it.

"Sorry, Belly Boo," I say, leaning over to give her a hug. "I have to get ready now. Go back to sleep, okay?"

"Okay," she says. "But what do I do when I wake up?"

"Well," I say, "you can have breakfast, and then play or read. Or ask Mom. I'll be home as soon as I can after my game, and then we will do something."

"Mom's not here," Belle says quietly.

"What?" I say. "Yes she is."

"No, she is not," Belle says.

I feel an electric shock of panic.

"What do you mean?" I ask. "Where is she?"

I need to get ready for my game and go. But I can't leave my sister here by herself.

"I don't know," Belle says. "But when I went to the bathroom, she wasn't there."

To get to the only bathroom in our apartment, we have to walk through our mom's room.

"When was that?"

Belle shrugs. "When it was dark. You were asleep."

I hurry through the main room, which is a living room and kitchen all in one, into our mom's room. And Belle's right—Mom definitely isn't there. And she isn't in the bathroom, either.

Belle and I are alone.

My mind starts racing. I feel like I'm spinning and nothing makes sense. Where is she? *Did she leave us alone all night? I can't leave Belle here by herself. I'm going to be late to my game.*

I realize I'm breathing hard and try to slow it down. Belle stares at me with huge eyes.

Okay. Obviously I can't leave Belle alone. So she'll have to come with me. I take a deep breath. I'm not sure where I'm going, and I don't want to have a seven-year-old tagging along. But we don't have a choice.

The longer I go without speaking, the more nervous Belle looks. I take another deep breath.

"Hey, Belly Boo! Do you still want to come to my soccer game?"

She smiles. "I get to come? Yes!"

Well, that's nice. I love how excited Belle gets about soccer games.

"Really?" I ask. "You really do want to come, all the way to Burlingame?"

"Yes!" she says again.

"Okay!" I say. "We have to eat breakfast fast!"

I look in the food cabinet and am relieved to find a box of cereal. But when I lift it up, it feels pretty light—just enough for us to split into two small bowls. At least there's milk in the fridge. I never know if there will be or not.

I look back in the cabinet to see if we have any snacks I can bring for Belle. She'll get hungry quickly after such a small breakfast. I find some old cheese crackers, and I try one to make sure it isn't stale. It is, a little, but not too bad. I fill a water bottle for her, find the short book we took out of the library a week ago, rip some blank pages from one of my school notebooks, and gather up a few crayons that aren't too badly broken.

I'm not sure if it's enough to keep Belle entertained, but it's all I can think of. I need something for her to do, because I don't think Coach is going to let her be his assistant, like Jayda did.

I pack it all into a small bag, slide that into my backpack, make sure Belle's dressed, and get us both out the door.

We hurry to our Muni stop and make it to the train station. We almost get on the wrong train, but I figure it out just in time. We miss the train I was hoping to take, but we get on the next one. We're still pretty much on schedule, and we can make it.

As long as everything else goes right.

11
YOU DON'T SCORE, YOU DON'T PLAY

WHEN BELLE AND I GET OFF THE TRAIN IN Burlingame, we walk quickly and then run the last three blocks to the field. We go as fast as Belle can go, and I feel like I'm dragging her, but she doesn't complain. We get there one minute past nine.

I find her a spot on the sideline, show her where the snacks and water and books and toys are, and sprint to where my team is gathered in front of one of the goals.

They haven't started warming up yet. I exhale all the way and try to catch my breath. A feeling of relief starts to wash over me.

Then Coach stops talking. Everyone stares at me.

"Well, look who decided to show up," he says. "Just so

you know, when I say get here an hour before the game, I mean it."

"Sorry, Coach," I say. I still haven't totally recovered my breath. "I had to take a bus and a train to get here, and my mom was gone, so my little sister—"

He cuts me off. "Please stop wasting our time."

I feel like I've been slapped in the face. I'm tempted to look away, down at my shoes, anywhere but at him, but somehow that feels like letting him win. So I swallow and keep my head up.

Before Coach starts going through the lineup, most of the girls on the team are still staring at me. The expressions on their faces range from annoyed at me to relieved that they aren't the one getting yelled at. Some look—if I'm not imagining it—sympathetic.

Their expressions all change quickly to looks of intense concentration as Coach names the starters. And the way he's talking—with long pauses to build up the drama—makes it seem like starting is a prize and sitting on the bench is punishment.

But there are sixteen girls on the team. There's no way *everyone* can start. I don't understand why he's trying to make the non-starters—including me—feel bad. It makes me mad.

All of us, starting or not, make a tight circle and put our hands in the middle for a team cheer. It's the club's signature "Don't mess with the best . . ." cheer. *Don't mess with the best, 'cause the best don't mess. Don't fool with the cool, 'cause the cool don't fool.*

It's my first time doing it, and it's just so . . . *braggy* that I can't say the words out loud and I just mouth them. It's a tiny protest that no one notices, but it makes me feel a little better.

I can hear Jayda's voice in my head saying, *There's no point in* talking *about how great you are. Just get out there and* be *great!* On my old team, we either yelled "One . . . two . . . three . . . REC!" or "Play hard! Have fun!"

After the cheer, I walk toward the bench with the other subs. But Coach grabs my arm and pulls me aside. I yank my arm back and scowl at him. It is *not* okay for him to grab me like that.

His teeth are gritted as he says, "You are here to score goals for us. *If* you get into the game, you better make that happen."

He strides over to the bench. I stand there, still on the field, with my mouth open.

For a moment, I don't move. I can't. And then I realize that he just absolutely confirmed what I have suspected since the moment I met him: he is a jerk.

But he's a jerk who I have to play for if I want to get to Nationals. I'm not sure how I feel about that.

Suddenly I have butterflies flitting around in my stomach. I'm more nervous for this game than I've ever been for any other game in my life. The stakes feel higher. My heart feels like it's beating way harder and faster than usual, but it's not in the usual good way.

The starters are in position and the ref is in the center of the field. I jog over to the bench and sit down at one end. Veronica, who is closest to me, shifts ever so slightly away.

I look at her.

She doesn't look at me.

The ref blows the whistle and the game starts. From the opening kickoff, I can tell that this is going to be a new level of soccer. The players are faster. The passes are crisper. The moves are trickier. The throw-ins go farther. The shots are harder.

It's . . . amazing. And as I watch, I start getting caught up in it. I feel more of the excitement that I usually feel during games.

Ten minutes go by, then fifteen. It's still 0–0. The Burlingame team is in our half of the field more often than we are in theirs, which surprises me. Our team is *supposed* to be better than every other team.

Coach keeps looking at us on the bench, making us think we might get a chance to play. I, for one, can't wait to get onto the field. He looks away, without calling any of us to go in.

Then Amelia, a defender on our team, steals the ball from a Burlingame player. She makes a great pass up the line to Ellie. Ellie controls it, makes a move around a defender, and passes it toward Apple, who is playing striker and is in the center of the field. It could have been a great pass, but Apple is on her heels, not on her toes. And the defender marking her is *fast*. I can see what's going to happen before it actually does.

The defender sees the pass coming and beats Apple to it. Apple tries to grab her shirt to slow her down—which is illegal, of course. But she doesn't get a good grip on it, and the defender easily moves away.

Now the defender has the ball in the middle of the field. Her teammates don't hesitate. One of the other team's strikers starts making a run, and the defender sends a perfect long ball over our defenders' heads. Their striker is fast, too, and she beats our defenders to the ball. She touches it a few times, then fires a shot toward the upper left corner of the goal.

But Liv is our keeper, and she's amazing. Even though

it was a brilliant shot, she knows exactly where the ball is going and manages to get a hand on it, tipping it up over the top crossbar.

No goal. But Burlingame gets a corner kick.

Coach is pacing, muttering under his breath, and looking at the bench. He signals to the ref that he wants to sub. He points toward Veronica and tells her to go in for Apple. "Do *not* let them beat you to the ball," he says. She nods and sprints onto the field. Apple looks surprised, then annoyed, but she jogs off the field. Slowly.

Coach looks mad, and I expect him to yell at Apple. But he doesn't say anything.

Apple sees the empty spot next to me on the bench and hesitates. Then she makes a face, spins around, and walks to the other end to squeeze in next to someone else. Whatever. More space for me.

Out on the field, Burlingame takes their corner kick. It's a good one, lofting up and coming down right in front of our goal. One of their strikers wins it in the air and tries to knock it into the goal. But Liv is there to save it. She pauses for a second, waves our defenders out of the box, and punts it way down the field to Veronica. But the fast defender is on her immediately, and although Veronica tries to keep possession, even shoving hard at the defender with both hands, the defender steals it.

The defender makes a pass through two of our defenders to a striker who's sprinting at full speed. Our defenders chase her, but their striker gets there first. She takes a few dribbles, then shoots with her left foot, hard and low toward the right goalpost. It would have been a sweet shot, but it misses by inches.

Goal kick.

Coach is now muttering and swearing under his breath, then yells orders at a bunch of our players, calling for a sub.

Finally he turns to me. "Get up, Alex," he says quietly. "Go in for Veronica at striker."

"Yes, Coach!" I say. I can feel the adrenaline shoot through me, all the way to my hands and feet. I'm ready. I may not like him, but I cannot wait to get into the game.

Then I think I hear him say something else. "You don't score, you don't play in the second half."

Wait. *What?*

I turn around and stare at him with my hands on my hips.

"What was that, Coach?" I ask, wondering if he'll say it more loudly.

He doesn't.

"Get me a goal," he says.

I'm going to try to get a goal, all right. But I'm going to get one for the team, and for me. So I tell him that. "I'll get our *team* a goal," I say.

I don't wait to see how he reacts.

12

HAT TRICK

AS I'M BOUNCING ON MY TOES, WAITING FOR the ref to wave me onto the field, I feel almost like I did before I went into my first-ever soccer game. It was at a place called Marina Green, where there is a huge row of small soccer fields on a big grassy space along the water of San Francisco Bay.

In the San Francisco microsoccer rec league, we played with small goals and no goalies, so all players from both teams chased the ball together. I figured out pretty quickly that if I ran as fast as I could to the ball and kicked it like I meant it, I could get it away from everyone else. Then I could chase it and dribble it and kick it into the goal. And I could do it again and again.

I scored twelve times in a row—really—before Jayda sent a new player onto the field to sub in for me.

Jayda gave me a fist bump and said, "Whoa! Alex! Is it true you just scored a whole bunch of goals? I saw the last one, and it was awesome."

"I scored twelve times!" I said.

"Well, that's . . . a quadruple hat trick!" Jayda said. "That's amazing."

I wrinkled my nose. "A what kind of hat?"

Jayda laughed. "A 'hat trick' is a funny name for when you score three goals in one game. But you scored *twelve* goals in one game. So that's four hat tricks, which you could also call a *quadruple* hat trick."

Then she told me, "I love how you're running so hard and getting the ball away from the crowd and taking it all the way to the goal." She grinned at me, and I felt like I was glowing with warmth from the inside. "And you know what?" she said. "There's something else you can do, especially once you've scored a few goals on the other team. Or twelve goals, in this case."

"What?" I asked.

"You can try to help your teammates get the ball and score, too!"

I considered that for a second. I wasn't sure how I felt about it. I liked scoring the goals myself.

Then Jayda told me something I've never forgotten. "It feels great to score, but it can feel just as good to pass to your teammates so they can score. Sometimes I think that feels even better, because your team gets to score and you get to help someone. The very best soccer players are *really* good at passing to their teammates. So what do you think? Do you want to try that, too?"

I thought about how it would feel to pass to Evie or Kiyomi, and to see how excited they would be if they scored.

And then I couldn't wait to get back into the game.

Just like I can't wait to get into the game now.

I sprint out into position. Liv takes the goal kick, and it's a long, hard ball that goes to midfield. Sera receives it, with time to turn and look upfield. "You've got me here, Sera," I call to her. She hesitates, looking for someone else to pass to, and almost loses it to a Burlingame midfielder. But at the last second, she sends a perfect pass my way. With a touch I'm past one defender, then I fake past another. I turn on my full speed and dribble toward the goal, drawing their keeper out of the net a bit. Then I shoot with my right foot, sending it over the keeper's head into the upper left corner.

Goal.

Less than a minute into my first time playing for Select. I can't help grinning.

Liv comes tearing up the field from the goal, yelling, "YES, ALEX! NICE *SHOT*!" She gives me a quick hug, and a few other players come over for high fives. On the bench, Apple and Veronica don't cheer at all, but I don't really care.

On the sidelines, the parents cheer, but Belle's cheers are definitely the loudest. I smile at her, and wave.

And just like that, we're up 1–0.

And then I score again on a corner kick, about thirty seconds before halftime. I take the kick, using my signature spin to curve it into the upper right corner of the goal. The other team's keeper almost gets a hand on it but doesn't quite touch it.

Now it's 2–0.

The ref blows the whistle for halftime, and as I jog from the field toward our bench, a few of my teammates— Amelia, Ellie, and Liv—jog with me, telling me what a great shot it was.

I feel a flash of pride. I'm new to the team, and this is the toughest game I've ever played, but I'm still making a difference out there.

As we approach the bench, Coach doesn't say

anything—or even look at me. Which is fine, I guess. Jayda never made a big deal about the person who scored a goal. She got more excited about the team effort that led to a goal.

But Coach doesn't mention that, either. He just rips on the players who made mistakes. (Except Apple, for some reason.) And then he finally looks at me. "Obviously, we have more sprinting to do at practice."

I feel blood rush to my cheeks and anger bloom in my chest. Was that directed at *me*? Even though I outran their defenders every time?

I don't have time to think much about it, though, because right then I feel a tug on my hand. I look, and there's Belle, with tears in her eyes.

"I'm sorry, Alex," she whispers. "But I have to go to the bathroom. I tried to hold it, but I have to go sooooo bad."

She's squeezing her legs together and squirming in a way that lets me know she *really* has to go. Poor kid. I have to take her to the bathroom, and I can't let her go alone. Last week everyone was talking about a girl in our neighborhood who had almost been kidnapped from a playground bathroom. I think I'd lose my mind if anything ever happened to Belle.

Of course, it never occurred to me that she would

have to use a playground bathroom in the middle of my soccer game. But here we are.

"Who is that?" Coach asks. "Get her out of here."

Anger flares in my chest again. "This is my little sister, and I have to take her to the bathroom," I say. Without waiting for Coach to respond, I grab Belle's hand and head toward the bathrooms we saw on the way in, near the playground.

I'm pretty sure I hear Coach say a word I'm not supposed to say, then he calls after me, "You leave now, and you're back on the bench!"

My face feels hot, but I don't turn around. I cannot believe this guy. He's going to bench me, after what I just did on the field?

But then I look down at Belle. Tears are streaming down her face. "I'm sorry, Alex," she says. "I have to go so bad."

"I know, Belly Boo. It's okay," I say. "Let's hurry."

I realize my hands are clenched into fists and that I didn't sound very nice when I told my sister to hurry. I take a deep breath. My sister comes before soccer. And you know what? If Coach wants to put me on the bench instead of letting me play, that's his loss.

We run as fast as Belle can and find an empty stall in

the bathroom. I stand guard outside. When she comes out, the look of relief on her face makes it all worth it, and I smile at her. Yup, taking care of my sister is way more important than getting playing time.

"Thanks, Alex," she says, and hugs me.

"I'm glad we made it," I say. "Now wash your hands and let's get to the field."

We run back and Belle settles down in her spot. The second half hasn't started yet, but our second-half starters—including Apple—are on the field. Apple turns and smirks at me as I sit on the bench.

Yeah, I don't know what her problem is. I try to ignore her.

"Don't worry about her," Amelia says as she sits down on the bench next to me. Right next to me, without shifting away at all. She played the whole first half, and played well. I'm surprised she's not starting the second half.

"I won't," I say, and I feel myself smile a little at her. "But what's up with her?"

"Well, first, she's kind of rude to everyone. She's one of those people who refuse to pronounce my last name correctly, you know? Like Huang is that hard to say," Amelia says, reaching up to pull her long, straight black hair into a tighter ponytail. "But what's up with her today? You scored against Burlingame. Twice. She hasn't even done it once. And we've never beaten them," Amelia explains.

"Wait," I say. "I thought Select always wins. Haven't you been undefeated, like, forever?"

"Who told you that?" Amelia asks. "We win a lot, but not every game. And definitely not against this team."

"Really," I say, trying to process this information. I thought Select was the best of the best. I thought they always won.

"Anyway, I'm surprised you're not in if he wants to keep winning this game," I say, nodding toward Coach. Amelia is probably our best defender.

"He got mad at me, so he benched me," she says.

"Mad at you? When? Why?" I ask. I feel a little guilty. Was I so caught up in my own anger at Coach that I didn't notice he got mad at other players, too?

Amelia hesitates.

"What happened?" I ask again.

"I said you were just helping your sister, and that I thought you were being nice. He told me I wouldn't be playing. Whatever," Amelia says, rolling her eyes. "I do think it's nice that you helped your sister. Where are your parents, though?"

I'm surprised to feel a kind of stinging in my chest

when she asks the question. "Ah . . . my mom . . . couldn't come," I mumble. I don't want to explain that she actually never came home last night, so we don't know where she is. Or that she works two jobs and can almost never come to my games. Or that my dad hasn't lived with us for years, and I almost never see him. "Thanks for saying that. Sorry Coach got mad at you," I say.

"It's okay," she says. "He'll figure out pretty soon that we should both be playing."

And before too long, he does.

Coach puts Amelia in first. Without her, the defense was having trouble clearing the ball out of our third of the field. As soon as Amelia goes in, that changes. Now our team is attacking, and the other team is trying to clear the ball.

But no matter how close we come, our strikers can't score. Which is fine. We're up 2–0. But I have a feeling Coach won't like it if we go the entire half with no goals.

Apple has been hustling hard on the field, and she's getting more and more frustrated. She keeps yelling at our teammates, and she's been called for shoving twice now. But I can also tell how badly Apple wants to score. The problem is that she's trying to do it on her own, and the Burlingame defense is too good for her to do that. She's taken a few shots, but they've been from way outside and missed the mark. In her desperation, she's getting even nastier to the other players.

The longer we go in the half without scoring, the more Coach paces and looks at me on the bench. I'm antsy, too. Technically, I'm sitting on the bench, but I can't stay still. I just want to get up and *play*.

Finally, with ten minutes to go, he subs me in for Apple. She refuses to look at me when I pass her on my way into the game.

Two minutes later, I have a chance. Ellie slips a pass through a gap in the defense and I race Burlingame's fastest defender to it. I get to the ball a split second before she does. She expects me to go right, but I go left and fire a hard shot with my left foot. It's almost perfect.

Almost.

But it deflects off the crossbar and one of their defenders sends it out, hard, over the sideline.

"Alex!" Coach yells. "What was that? When you get a shot like that, you do not miss!"

Which makes some of the parents think it's okay to yell at me, too. (News flash: it's *not*.)

I hear a few dads yelling things like, "Come on! You have to shoot it *on goal*!"

As if the team has been shooting on goal all day and I'm the first to be slightly—*slightly*—off-target.

Amelia grabs the ball. She has an incredible throw-in, so she often sprints up the field to take throw-ins on her side. Her throw clears two of their defenders. I run onto it, touch it past a third defender, and shoot with my right. Low and hard, into the right corner.

Goal.

I don't jump up and down. I just glare at the dads who yelled at me for missing—they aren't saying anything now. But my teammates run to high-five me.

My third goal of the game. A hat trick.

I smile, thinking of Jayda telling me what a hat trick was, back when I was five and a half.

And then I think about what she told me next, about how good it feels to help a teammate score.

With about thirty seconds to go, I steal the ball from a Burlingame player and dribble past another one. From the corner of my eye, I see Ellie streaking toward the goal. She's *fast*. I send the ball through the space between Burlingame's last two defenders, judging that Ellie will get there just as the ball does.

She does. She controls the ball with two touches, then fires it well to the left of the goalie, into the back of the net.

She sprints back to me at full speed—which, for her, means incredibly fast—and comes barreling into me with her arms outstretched for a hug. "Sweet pass!" she says.

"Sweet goal!" I say back, feeling a surge of happiness.

It *does* feel just as good to assist a teammate as it does to score a goal yourself.

Maybe even better.

13

AREN'T YOU LUCKY TO BE HERE

WHEN THE REF BLOWS THE WHISTLE TO END the game, the parents on the sideline and all the girls on my team erupt into cheers. The girls are high-fiving each other and giving each other hugs.

Liv, Amelia, and Sera are high-fiving and hugging me, too.

I get caught up in it for a second, but mostly I just want to see how Belle is doing.

I jog toward her on the sideline, where she has stayed so patiently by herself for the whole game (minus the bathroom trip, of course). She has packed up all her stuff and tried to put it back into the bag, although a few things are hanging out as she carries it toward me.

She has a huge smile on her face. When I get to her, she throws her arms around me.

"Alex!" she shouts, her face buried in my jersey. "It was fun to watch you play!"

I put my arms around her, which feels even better than winning. It's a nice feeling, having someone you love hug you after your game. And to feel like someone is happy to be at your game watching you, with no expectations. Belle is glad we won, sure, but she would have been just as happy to see me if we'd lost.

"Thanks, Belly Boo," I say. "And thanks for coming. It was fun to have you here. Ready to get going?"

"Wait, Alex," she says, and points to a spot just down the sideline, where parents from my team are setting out more snacks than I have ever seen in one place. There are juice boxes, cut fruit, cookies decorated to look like soccer balls, individual bags of Pirate's Booty, a cooler full of Popsicles and ice cream sandwiches, fruit snacks, granola bars, and cupcakes. It's all arranged on a folding table covered with a paper tablecloth in red and black, our team colors, and there's a **SELECT** banner pinned to it.

I've seen other teams have snacks after games, although I've never actually experienced it. But this . . . this is on another level. I look around to see if some other teams are coming, or if someone is having a birthday party or something.

Nope.

It's just postgame snacks for our team.

Belle and I watch in amazement as the girls from my team, and a lot of their younger siblings, gather around the table. The younger kids take the most food, loading up on sweets while their parents are distracted. My teammates are mostly more restrained; they each take one or two things, although not everyone finishes. Coach is standing over the food and watching what they all take with a pinched look on his face.

The moms sip on cans of sparkling water. A few of the dads have cupcakes or cookies. But even after everyone has taken what they want, there's barely a dent in what's there.

Once the crowd around the table has dispersed a little, I lead Belle over so she can choose something. I take some fruit and a bag of Pirate's Booty. Then, just because I can, I grab a cookie, too. Belle stands there, staring at everything, her mouth open.

"Do you want a snack, Belly Boo?" I ask, and nudge her toward the table.

She looks up at me, her eyes as wide as saucers. "It's

really okay?" she asks. I look around to confirm. Yes, the younger siblings of my teammates have definitely loaded up on treats.

"It's really okay," I say.

Belle approaches the table, looking like a kid at a candy store. We don't have extra snacks at home. Sometimes we don't even have stuff for breakfast or lunch. She reaches out to take a strawberry, then pulls her hand back. Then she reaches toward a cookie but pulls back again.

"Just take what you want, Belly," I say. "Go ahead. That's what it's there for."

"But can I have a strawberry *and* a cookie?" she asks, shocked.

"*Yes,*" I say, again looking at all the siblings with full plates, and the heaps of excess food on the table.

So she takes both. And bites right into the strawberry. A little red juice dribbles onto her chin.

At that moment, one of the moms—I think it's Apple's mom—comes over to us. Her smooth blond hair is practically sparkling, and she's wearing fancy workout clothes, although I can't imagine her ever actually working out in them.

"These snacks are for the players," she says. "But if your little sister wants some, I *suppose* it's fine." As if she's doing Belle a huge favor. As if a whole bunch of other siblings and parents haven't taken food, too. Belle freezes, her mouth full of strawberry. She can sense the suggestion that she's done something wrong, and she doesn't understand.

Neither do I. I can feel my cheeks turning red.

Then the mom says, "Are you Alex? How *nice* to meet you! This"—she pauses and kind of waves her hands around—"must seem very different from what you're used to." Maybe she's talking about the snacks, or the nice field in a town outside the city, or the team in general. I don't know. Then she says, "Aren't you lucky to be here." She purses her lips in a half smile, shakes her head, and walks away.

Belle looks at me with wide eyes and her mouth still full.

"It's okay, Belly Boo. You can eat your snacks," I say.

She nods and slowly starts chewing the strawberry again. After she gulps it down, she asks, "Why did that lady say you're lucky to be here?"

I watch as Apple's mom walks away. She's heading toward her car, talking on her phone, with Apple trailing a few steps behind.

"I don't know, Belly. Because I get to be on this team? Not everyone makes it," I say.

"Oh," Belle says, looking confused. "But . . . but I think *they* are lucky. That you play on their team."

I smile.

Sometimes the seven-year-old point of view is really good to hear. And I know she's right.

14

DID YOU WIN?

WHEN BELLE AND I GET BACK TO OUR APART-
ment after the game, our mom is there. She's lying on
the couch, eyes closed, with the TV on. At first, I'm
relieved to see that she's come home.

She doesn't move when we walk in. I see the re-
mote on the floor and use it to turn off the TV. The
silence must startle her because she wakes and sits up,
dazed.

Then she sees us. "Hi, girls," she says, smiling. "Were
you at the rec center?"

I stare at her in disbelief. "Mom," I say sharply. "We
were in *Burlingame*."

The smile fades from her face. "You were where? But

why were you . . . oh," she says, and her shoulders slump. "I forgot, didn't I?"

"You forgot my first game. For Select. When I got up this morning, you weren't even here to watch Belle. Where *were* you?" I finish angrily.

She buries her face in her hands for a moment, then looks up at us. "I'm so, so sorry, girls. Yesterday was a long day. It's been . . ." She trails off with a sigh, and tears come into her eyes. "It's been hard, lately. I've been trying to make more money, and Xander said I could drive his UrbanGrub shift last night." UrbanGrub is a food-delivery service. I didn't know Xander did that. I don't know much about Xander, come to think of it. "By the time I finished," my mom continues, "I was wiped out. I didn't want to wake you girls, so I stayed over at his place."

I was starting to feel sorry for her—right up until the part where she mentioned where she was when she didn't come home.

"So you left two kids alone all night and stayed with your boyfriend? You're not supposed to do that," I say. "You should always come home."

She nods. And then hangs her head. "You're right," she mumbles. "I'm sorry. I promise . . ." She trails off again, and I'm glad she doesn't finish that thought. "I'm sorry," she repeats.

"When you weren't here this morning, I had to take Belle with me all the way to Burlingame. I wasn't even sure where I was going, but we made it."

Our mom smiles. "Of course you did. You can do anything," she says, and the sound of pride in her voice makes some of my anger go away. "You know that's why I wanted you to join this team, right? Because you can do anything, including getting a soccer scholarship to go to college. I think this team will help you."

I sigh. Suddenly I'm just tired. I flop onto the couch and shrug. "I don't know, Mom. It's tough."

And then she finally asks me about the game. "Well, did you win?"

It's the question she always asks me after a game. The only thing she ever says to me after a game. I tell myself it's because she never played sports and can't think of better questions. And she doesn't know that the best thing for a parent to say—after actually *watching* a game—is "I love watching you play." That's what Kiyomi's mom and dad always said to her. They didn't care if we won or not.

My mom first asked "Did you win?" after my first game, when she came to pick me up at the rec center afterward. She was pushing Belle in a stroller, and she looked like she was in a hurry. When she saw me, she said, "Come on. Let's get going."

As we were walking, I said, "The game was fun!"

She had been looking at her phone, and she looked down at me, distracted.

"Oh. Good." Then the question: "Did you win?"

"No one wins in microsoccer," I explained. "But, Mom—"

"Okay, well, at least you didn't lose," she said, cutting me off. "Alexa, can you walk a little faster? I have a lot to get done."

When we got home, my dad was already there. He was lying on the couch, which was the only furniture we had in that room, and the TV was on.

He muted it for a second and looked at my mom. "You going to the store today? There's nothing to eat," he said.

"Sorry," she said. "Yes, I'm going. I didn't think you'd be home yet."

"Rough night last night. Tough workout this morning. I'm wiped out," he said. "Keep them quiet." He nodded his head toward Belle and me.

I didn't talk to my dad much, but since he liked sports, I decided to try.

"I had my first soccer game today!" I announced.

He kind of snorted and laughed at the same time. "*You* had a *soccer* game?" he said, as if it were a really silly idea. "You don't even play soccer."

"Yes, I do," I said.

"Well, did you win?" he asked.

"It doesn't matter who wins in microsoccer," I said. "But I scored—"

He cut me off. "That's stupid," he said. "Of course it matters who wins."

The "Did you win?" question has bugged me ever since.

But my mom seems genuinely interested this time, so I swallow and answer her. "Yes, we won."

She smiles. "That's great," she says, and she doesn't rush to change the subject, so I keep talking.

"And I had an assist and three goals, but Coach didn't give me much playing time. And I don't think he really wants to, but I don't know why."

"Don't be silly," my mom says, getting up and stretching. "Why wouldn't he want you to play?"

"I really don't know," I say.

"Well, be nice to him and don't cause trouble," she says. "Then maybe he'll treat you better."

I tilt my head to the side and squint at her. This is how she thinks about dealing with people who don't treat her well—my dad, Xander, and probably lots of other people. My mom may be right about some things. But I know she's wrong about this.

15

WHAT DID HE JUST SAY?

AT THE FIRST SELECT PRACTICE AFTER WE beat Burlingame, something is different. It's as if Coach had been holding back during our earlier practices. He doesn't seem to be holding back now.

When we all gather around him at the beginning of practice, he launches right into a string of criticisms about how we played.

"That game was ridiculous. It took you almost an entire half to score your first goal. You weren't winning balls. You weren't being aggressive. You weren't *trying*."

I don't know what to think. I was definitely trying. And so were my teammates, from what I could tell.

And then he says something bizarre. So bizarre I think I must have misheard him.

"When you play a team as weak as that, I expect you to crush them. Those girls weren't soccer players," he says.

What did he just say? I don't understand, and I feel my heart thumping. We played a really good game, against a strong team. So I ask, "What do you mean, they 'weren't soccer players'? They were good soccer players."

If fire could actually come out of a person's eyes, it would be happening when Coach looks at me. He squints at me dangerously, and my jaw snaps shut. "Do *not* interrupt me," he says.

I don't say anything else, but I don't look away. I shouldn't need to—calling out his ridiculous comment felt important, somehow. Out of Coach's line of sight, I see Liv and Amelia nodding at me.

After that, practice is intense. We do drill after drill. If I don't do something perfectly, Coach lets me know it. And then we do sprint after sprint. Whenever Jayda had our team run sprints, she reminded us that working on fitness at practice meant we would be stronger and faster in our games. It was always positive.

This kind of feels like punishment. Although why we're being punished after beating Burlingame for the first time ever is beyond me.

There's no encouragement. Coach never tells us we are working hard, or to keep it up. He just keeps telling us to go again. Another Select coach, Tim, who sometimes helps with our practices, comes over while we're sprinting.

"Working them hard today, Coach?" he says.

"If they run enough, maybe they'll stop playing like girls," Coach says. Again I think, *What did he just say?* But I heard him, all right. He's coaching a really talented team of girls, and yet he has no respect for girls.

Both Coach and Tim laugh.

My blood boils.

I'm not the only one who heard all of this. Liv did, too, apparently, because she says, "Play like girls? They *wish* they could play like we do."

I catch her eye, and she smirks at me. I nod back at her with a smile.

Because she is so right.

16

SHE'S AN IDIOT

MY SECOND SELECT GAME IS A HOME GAME, SO
I just have to take my usual bus to the fields where we
practice. And after that first game, when our mom wasn't
there in the morning, Belle asked if she could come to all
of my games. Of course I said yes.

We arrive an hour and a half before the game—that's
thirty minutes *before* Coach wants the players there. I'm
not going to give him another reason to bench me.

I'm feeling oddly flat and unexcited about the game,
which has never happened before. I usually wake up on
game days with excited butterflies and tingling fingers.
But this morning I woke up feeling like I had a pit in
my stomach.

Like I was dreading the game.

But that can't have been right. I don't dread soccer.

We have plenty of time to use the bathroom and make sure Belle has everything she needs, so I won't have to leave the field. I sit with Belle on her blanket and read to her for a few minutes, trying to keep her warm. It's a super-foggy San Francisco morning, with mist so thick we can barely see the other side of the field.

When the other players start showing up, I stand. "Okay, Belly Boo. Time for me to go. You good?" I ask.

She nods. Then she pulls my hand and motions for me to bring my head right down next to hers. "I promise I won't have to pee again!" she whispers. Then she says, "Can you score a goal today?"

I smile. "I'll try," I say. Belle's excitement starts to get me excited, and I feel lighter as I jog over to join my teammates. When I'm almost there, I turn around and wave at Belle. She waves back and smiles.

That's all I need. I can't help but smile back.

My teammates are passing and dribbling as they wait for our official warm-up to start. Everyone is already paired off. So I grab my ball—my lucky rec center ball, the one I've had since Jayda let me take it home after my first season—and start juggling.

For some reason we never juggle at Select practice.

Jayda always said it was a great way to work on touch, but I figure maybe it isn't serious enough for Coach. (I have since learned that he actually doesn't know how to juggle, so maybe that's what's up. But anyway.)

Since I've started playing with Select, I haven't felt like practicing juggling at home, so I haven't set a new juggling record in a few months. My record is up to 1,352, but my new goal is to get to fifteen hundred.

It usually takes me a few tries to get into a good rhythm. On my first attempt today, I get 72. Then 126. Then 368. When the ball drops after 368, I look up and see that some of my teammates have stopped what they are doing and are staring at me. At first I'm confused, because it doesn't seem like a big deal to me, but 368 is a lot of juggles. Liv is the first one to say something.

"Alex, that was amazing!"

My cheeks get warm from the inside and I know they are turning red. I smile. "Oh," I say. "Thanks."

"How did you *do* that?" Amelia asks.

There's no trick, of course. "Just practice," I say. "My old coach, Jayda, taught me when I was little."

Amelia's eyes widen. "Jayda Rodman? Was *she* your coach?" Her voice is full of admiration. Before I have a chance to ask how she knows about Jayda, we hear Coach's voice.

"Stop talking and get over here—now," he says.

We all zip it immediately and sprint over to him. He has his hands on his hips.

"You are playing a mediocre team today," he says, not at all quietly, as he glances over at our opponents. We look, too. The team just arrived, and they're talking and laughing as they make their way from the parking lot and across the field to the players' side. The club is called Girls Together. Their coach is walking with them, also talking and laughing.

She looks . . . nice. She kind of reminds me of Jayda. With a pang of sadness, I think of my old team. They have a game today, too, and I am rooting for them.

Coach is not impressed.

"And their coach, is . . . well," he says, then pauses and glances over again at the other team. "She's not even mediocre."

I cringe, because he says this loudly, in a voice as sharp as a tack. And she isn't far away—Girls Together is setting up a bench about fifteen yards away from us. I look at their coach. Obviously, just seeing someone can't tell you much about her, but she looks like a good soccer coach. And it looks as if her players actually like her.

If she heard what Coach just said about her, then she's doing a good job ignoring it.

"I am expecting a bigger win this week than last week," Coach continues. "You should destroy this team. And if you don't . . . ," he says, then pauses again. Coach likes the dramatic pauses. "Practice will not be fun next week."

Ha, I think. I almost snort out loud. As if practices with Coach are ever fun.

Just then, Apple strolls over to where Coach is talking to us. She doesn't look like she's in any rush. My heart starts pounding. Even though I'm not a huge fan of Apple, I'm not looking forward to how mean Coach is going to be. I hold my breath as I wait to hear what he will say to her as she joins us and . . .

Nothing.

He says nothing.

Not directly to Apple, anyway. He just tells us to get into groups of four to play three-versus-one triangle keep-away, and tells Liv and Scarlett, the backup keeper, to warm each other up.

A combination of confusion and frustration makes me feel like my head is going to explode. It isn't that I *want* him to get mad at another player—not even Apple. But it doesn't make sense. He gets upset at pretty much everything—*especially* when players are late. I think of how mad he was when I showed up late last week, and I grit my teeth.

I fight the urge to say something. Although I've decided I'm going to keep speaking up to Coach when I need to, I know this isn't one of those times. I certainly don't want to call out my teammate for being late.

I'm going to focus on the game.

I run to join a group to start playing keep-away. As we're playing, I see the coach from the other team walk over to Coach. She doesn't look thrilled to be talking to him, but she reaches out her hand to shake—as coaches do before most games, and as I saw Coach do last weekend with the guy who was coaching the Burlingame team. Coach stares at her for a second, then shakes her hand limply, like he did to me the first time we met. I wonder if his palm is sweaty again today.

It probably is, because she wipes her hand on her soccer pants immediately. Then, as Coach stalks away from her, she shakes her head, shrugs her shoulders, and goes back to her team.

Before the game starts, I find Liv and whisper, "What's up with the coach from the other team? Does Coach know her or something?"

She gives a little laugh. "Oh, he knows her. He hates

her. She coached for Select, for, like, five minutes. She was the only female coach he ever hired, and she quit almost immediately. A few of her players left with her."

I look at her again. She's leaning forward, listening to something one of her players is saying. She seems interested and concerned. She's paying attention. She reminds me of Jayda more than ever.

"Oh, and . . . why . . . ?"

I don't finish the thought.

Liv looks at me. "Why what?" she asks.

I glance around to make sure no one is listening. "Why doesn't he mind if Apple is late?" I ask.

"He does," she says. "But her dad basically paid for everything to help start this club, back when her older brother was our age. So Coach doesn't say anything to Apple."

"Got it," I say, trying to imagine what it would be like to have a parent with enough money to start a whole new soccer club for me. I wonder if Coach would treat me differently if I did.

Just then I hear the referee blow her whistle from midfield. The captain from the other team runs right over to the ref. Apple, who is our team captain this week, stops to get a drink from her water bottle and redo her ponytail while the other captain and the ref wait. Finally, she walks out to midfield.

I recognize this referee. She's younger than a lot of refs, but she's been working San Francisco games for at least two seasons, and she reffed a few of my games with my old team. I like her because she's really fair, and she always explains her calls if a player doesn't understand. The grumpy old refs never do that.

From the look on Apple's face, I guess that the coin toss doesn't go her way. She walks back to our bench, rolling her eyes.

"They have the kickoff," she says. "And I do not like this ref."

I raise my eyebrows. I can't imagine going through life not liking people if I didn't get exactly what I wanted all the time. I guess I wouldn't really like anyone, in that case.

Coach looks up from his whiteboard at the ref, then waves his hand dismissively, as if the ref is a fly that he's swatting away. He looks back down.

Apple is in the starting lineup; I am not.

From the opening kickoff, the game is tight. Our team plays hard, sprints fast, and it feels like every play is urgent. But it's also kind of messy. We aren't connecting on passes, and we're having trouble getting into the other team's third of the field. They are attacking, and we are clearing the ball away from our goal, but always into a crowd of their players.

Meanwhile, the other team is much more relaxed than we are. Their passes are on point. They're moving to open space. They're flowing. Luckily, Liv is stopping every shot they take, and sending the ball deep into the other half with her awesome punts.

One punt goes far over the heads of their defenders, who have pulled up, trying to keep the ball in our half. Apple, who's playing striker, hasn't noticed how far up they are. And she's still hanging out about ten yards into their half, putting her about ten yards offside. I see that and call to her from the bench to check her position, but either she doesn't hear me or she ignores me. The ball goes over her head, too, but she's closest to it and she has a ten-yard advantage on the nearest defender.

Apple gets control of the ball and starts dribbling fast toward the other team's goal. It looks like a pure breakaway. Like she has a really good chance of scoring.

Except for one thing.

When she got the ball, she was indeed offside. Way off. The ref blows her whistle, but Apple doesn't stop.

The ref blows her whistle again, a few times. Sharply and shrilly. Finally Apple stops, turns around, and says, "Are you kidding me? You took away my advantage!"

As if the ref blew her whistle because of something the other team had done.

"Offside," the ref calls, jogging toward Apple so she can grab the ball and set it for the other team's free kick.

"*What?*" Apple practically screeches, with her hands on her hips and her head tilted to the side.

"You were offside," the ref says firmly.

"Are you *blind*?" Coach yells from the sideline.

Even given everything I've heard Coach say to me, and to other players, and about other players, this shocks me. Apple was clearly offside. No question. If I had been that far off, Coach would have been mad at me, and he would have been right that I'd made a mistake.

I know coaches argue with refs sometimes, but they usually argue about close calls. Now Coach is just lying, and *everyone* knows it, even if they aren't speaking up. But why is he doing this? To try to intimidate the ref?

The ref takes a few steps toward the sideline and says calmly, "I'm not blind. She was offside. By a lot. I saw it, and the linesperson saw it. Anyone who was paying attention saw it."

She spins around and motions for everyone to get ready for the free kick.

"I'm going to let the league know about this," Coach says through gritted teeth.

"Go ahead," the ref says over her shoulder. She waits a second for everyone to get lined up, then blows her whistle.

"Pull up. Pull *up*!" Coach calls to our defenders, who look confused. They're right to be confused. This isn't the right field position for an offside trap. They should be marking players, not pulling up. They look at each other. *"Pull up now!"* Coach yells again.

So they do, leaving several players from the other team offside. But the other team's players are paying attention, and they pull back to be even with our defenders, just as a player from the other team takes the kick. It sails perfectly over our defenders' heads, and their fastest striker beats our defender to it. She controls it and has a clean breakaway—just like Apple thought she had a few minutes ago, but without breaking any rules.

The other team's striker is not only fast, she's also a great dribbler. She keeps the ball close and in control, and our defender, Arden, can't quite catch her.

"Do something!" Coach calls. And Arden seems to

know what he means, because she blatantly trips their player, who goes down *hard*.

The ref blows her whistle loudly and flashes a yellow card at Arden.

Coach starts arguing with the ref, but I'm just watching the player from the other team, who hasn't gotten up yet. Her coach runs out to help her, concerned and kind.

Finally, the player gets up slowly. I think she had the wind knocked out of her, but it looks like she's okay.

The other team gets a direct kick. As they should. And part of me even wants them to score.

Their strongest shooter steps up to take it, and the shot is perfect. Liv is so good that she almost stops it, but she only gets one glove on the ball, and it skids off the tips of her fingertips into the corner of the net.

Now we're down 0–1. And Coach is raging mad. I hear him spit out, *"She's an idiot!"* That's followed by a string of words that any kid would get in major trouble for saying.

The ref, still calm, walks over and flashes another yellow card, this time at Coach.

"If you call me names again, you're out of here," she says. Then she turns and walks away to restart the game.

Coach's eyes look like they're firing bullets at her. But he does not call her another name.

We are still down 0–1 at halftime. Coach doesn't start me in the second half, but it's as if he just did that to make a point, because he puts me into the game a minute later, subbing me in for Apple.

I'm so happy to be on the field instead of on the bench that I put all Coach's nastiness out of my head. I hustle like crazy from the first second I'm in the game, and quickly intercept a pass from one of the other team's defenders. It's incredible how many balls you can steal if you just step up your hustle.

Once I get the ball, I don't waste any time. I take two touches toward the other team's goal, and then before any of their defenders can get in my way, I send the ball down the line to the spot where I know Ellie will be in a few seconds. Sure enough, she comes flying toward the ball, taps it out of reach of their last defender, and fires a shot. It goes *just* over the crossbar, but that's okay. The momentum and energy on the field has totally shifted.

"Keep the pressure on!" I call to my teammates, as the other team sets up for a goal kick. I noticed from the bench that their goalie doesn't have a super-strong kick, and that more than half the time, she sends a pass to one of her defenders rather than clearing the ball. Just like the other team's goalie from my last rec league game.

Like I was then, I'm ready for it now.

The goalie fakes a kick and passes it.

I race toward the ball and get there just as the defender makes contact. I come in for a hard tackle and win the ball, bumping it goalside of the defender. I chase it, take two dribbles, and shoot hard. This one comes in just under the crossbar. And we are tied, 1–1.

Later that half, I repeat my first pass to Ellie up the sideline. She's there, like clockwork, and she shoots again. But this time it's low and to the corner, and she scores.

Now we're up 2–1, and I have a goal and an assist. When Liv high-fives me, she whispers, "Thanks for showing everyone that we don't need to cheat to win."

No one scores again, so the final is 2–1.

It's not enough for Coach. Not even close. When he talks to us after the game, he keeps repeating the score.

"Two to one, huh? You beat a *Girls Together* team *two to one*?" His voice is dismissive as he says the club name.

Okay. We get it. He doesn't like the score. But this obsession with the score is over-the-top. Obviously I know we are trying to win games—which we just *did*— but he is way too focused on the score.

I like winning. And sure, I like winning by a lot. But I've never been *that* worried about the final score. In the microsoccer league, teams aren't even supposed to keep score. There are no standings, or first-place trophies. It's all about fun.

But anyway, even though we weren't supposed to keep score, at the end of my first microsoccer game, every kid on our team knew what the score was: 19–1.

When the game ended, the players from our field ran over to Jayda and the players from the other field and announced, "We won!"

Jayda smiled, then said, "Did you have fun?"

"Yes!" I said. "We won nineteen to one!"

"Well . . . ," Jayda said, "the thing is, we don't keep score in microsoccer. I'm not sure what the score was on your field, or on the other field. But I do know that I saw you all playing hard and helping each other."

"It *was* nineteen to one," Camilla insisted.

"Okay," Jayda laughed. "Maybe it was. I know it's hard not to keep track of the score. But we are here to have fun, and to learn to play, and to make sure that no one leaves feeling too sad about losing. If you want to keep score in your head, you can do that."

Of course, when we got older and graduated from microsoccer into youth soccer, we started keeping score. Still, Jayda never got hung up on the score of a game.

But I have a new coach now.

After he's done ranting at us about winning by only one goal, Coach walks away from us, then turns over his shoulder and says, "Don't forget your cheer." Ugh. I put my hand in the middle of the circle with the other girls, but I don't even pretend to say the words.

The other team gives a cheer, too, although they are cheering for us. "Good game, Select!" they shout. And the other coach even stops to tell me I played well.

"So did your team," I say, meaning it.

She smiles. "Thanks," she says, then adds, "Try not to let him get to you." I'm surprised by this, but the few seconds we spend together feel like a safe space, somehow. I feel warm inside. But it would be strange to tell her that, so I just nod, and she walks away.

For the first time in my soccer career, I find myself thinking a lot about the score after the game is over, wishing it had been different. I wish my team hadn't won a game against a nice coach like her.

And I feel embarrassed to be part of a team with a coach who acts like Coach does.

17

1,548

EVEN AFTER WE GET HOME FROM THE GAME,
I'm still cringing inside whenever I think about the way
Coach treated the ref and the other coach.

I know why I decided to join this team. I want to
play soccer at the highest level possible. I want to be on
a team that can go all the way to Nationals. But I have
a nagging feeling that doing it with Coach leading us
won't ever feel quite right to me. It won't feel like home,
the way playing for Jayda's team did. And suddenly I
really want to go to my happy place.

"Hey, Belly Boo!" I say. "Want to go to the rec center
and learn to juggle?"

"Yes!" she shouts, and runs into our room. She comes
out smiling and holding my soccer ball, the one Jayda

let me "borrow" years ago. "Can I practice with this one?" she asks.

"Of course," I say. "It's the best juggling ball around."

Disliking Coach shouldn't get in the way of all the things that are fun about soccer. I'm starting to understand what Jayda said to me right before I joined Select—not to forget how much I love soccer.

I got hooked on juggling when I was little, after I told Jayda I wished I could play every day. The next day, she taught me about juggling.

"It's one of the best ways to work on your touch when you don't have much space, or other people to play with," she said. First she taught me how to juggle on my thighs, and then on my feet. "It's all great practice," she said, "but once you get the rhythm down, concentrate on juggling with your feet."

Then she told me that once I got the hang of it, I could keep track of how many I got in a row. "It's like a competition with yourself, just for you, as a way to challenge yourself," she said.

"Can you do it?" I asked.

"I can," she said with a smile.

"Will you show me?"

"Sometime I will," she said. "But for now . . ."

"Please? *Please?*" I begged. I had a feeling it would be cool to watch her juggle.

I was right.

She pulled the ball close to her with her foot, then looked at me and said, "One thing, Alex. I'll show you some juggling, but don't expect to be able to do this right away, okay?"

"Okay," I said.

"But also, Alex? If you keep practicing, you *will* be able to do this someday. Probably better than I can!"

I nodded.

She drew the ball back with the bottom of her right foot, popped it up with the tops of her toes, and started juggling. Back and forth, from one foot to the other. Ten times, twenty times, fifty . . . so many times I lost count. Occasionally she'd do two or three on one foot, then get into a back-and-forth rhythm again.

I just watched. I was mesmerized. It was both the coolest and most soothing thing I'd ever seen. After a few minutes she flicked the ball up and caught it, then handed it back to me.

"There you go," she said.

"Did you count?" I asked.

She grinned. "I did. I always do," she said.

"How many did you get?"

"Two hundred," she said.

"Could you get more?" I asked.

"Yes, I could," she said. "But that felt like enough for today."

"How many could you get?"

"A lot," she said, laughing. "But now it's your turn."

I wanted to do it with my feet, like Jayda did. It wasn't easy. I couldn't pop it up with my foot like she could, so I started by dropping it from my hands onto one of my feet. Most times I only got one or two juggles before missing.

But once that day, I got five in a row.

And I knew if I kept trying, soon I'd get more.

Jayda let me "borrow" a soccer ball from the rec center to take home so I could practice every day. By the end of the spring season, I could get nine juggles in a row. Over the summer, I got it up to fourteen. By the time I was nine, I was setting and breaking new records almost every week: 132 . . . 278 . . . 435 . . . 771 . . . 926. That was my record for a long time.

I finally broke one thousand earlier this year, at the last practice before the last game of my spring season. I got to 1,352.

I haven't tried to break my record since.

But that's going to change today.

Belle and I walk hand in hand to the rec center. Jayda isn't there, which is a bummer. She's coaching my old team at a game, and no one is sure when she'll be back.

We find a space in the courtyard, and I show Belle how to start juggling, first on her thighs and then on her feet, just like Jayda showed me when I was little. Belle mostly gets one juggle, then sends the ball flying on her second touch. The next time she tries, it goes up and over her head, bouncing somewhere behind her.

"This is *hard*, Alex," she says, but she still giggles every time she loses the ball.

"I know. Just try again," I say. "Every time it drops, try again. I had to try again so many times. But now I can do it!"

"Will you show me?" Belle asks.

"Sure," I say. She runs to grab the ball from where it rolled under a bench, drops it, and passes it to me. "Nice pass," I say. "I can tell you've been practicing that."

"Yup!" she says proudly. "Now you juggle!"

I flick the ball up with my foot and juggle it about twenty-five times, then let it drop. "There you go," I say. "You just have to get into a rhythm."

"Alex," she says, "I know you can do more than that. Come on! Try to break your record!"

Belle and Jayda are the only ones who know about my record, and how much I like to keep breaking it.

"Really?" I say. "It might take a while. And I want you to keep practicing!"

"Try!" she says. "I want to see. Please?"

"Okay," I say. I stare at the ball for a moment and take a deep breath. There's a kind of calm zone I have to be in if I want to get a lot of juggles, and for a moment it's just me, the ball, and a stillness in the air. Then I flick the ball up and start.

After about fifty juggles, including one where I almost lost it, I settle in. I'm in the zone.

One hundred.

Two hundred.

Three hundred.

And still going. I tune out everything around me. The noise from the rec center, and from the street. Everything that's been bothering me about soccer and Coach. I'm not thinking about anything but the ball on my feet.

Eight hundred . . . nine hundred . . . one thousand . . .

I get to twelve hundred and realize that I'm within striking distance of my record. That's the point where it's especially important to stay calm. I make sure I'm breathing steadily, and I try not to think about the record.

Thirteen hundred . . . fourteen hundred . . . fifteen hundred . . .

At 1,548, I tap the ball a little too hard, and it comes down just out of reach.

A new record. I look at Belle, who runs over to give me a hug. And then I hear cheering from across the courtyard. It's Jayda and most of my former teammates.

They all run over to me and give me high fives.

"Woo-hoo!" Jayda says with a huge smile. "That was *amazing*. We got back right as you were starting. Was it fifteen hundred and fifty?"

"Nope, fifteen forty-eight," I say. "But it's my new record."

"Oh, I know!" Jayda says. "You broke my record, too!"

"I did?" I say, wondering if she's a little bothered by that. But of course she's not.

"You did," she says, her grin getting even bigger. "Just like I knew you would."

My old teammates start chattering about juggling and their game—which they won, not that I was going to ask about that right away—and it feels so right to be with them. I keep hugging Kiyomi, and I realize how much I've missed her. She doesn't go to my school, and we haven't even been texting much. But she whispers, "Can you come over later?" and I nod, and it's like our time apart never happened. I wonder if being with my new team could ever feel this good. I could maybe see it happening with my new teammates. But I don't know that it's going to happen with Coach there.

18

PART OF THE TEAM

A FEW WEEKS LATER, WE HAVE A GAME AT A field in San Mateo. For anyone getting a ride in a car, it's a forty-minute trip. For me it will be an hour and a half, first on a BART train and then on the Caltrain. From there it's a mile walk to the field.

Actually, it ends up being a little more than a mile, because Belle and I get kind of lost. But by now I know to plan ahead. It's a one o'clock game, so we're supposed to arrive by noon, but even with our detour, we get there just after eleven a.m.

I'm glad we do. While it's cold and foggy in the city, the weather is warm and sunny in San Mateo, and there's a walking trail in a loop around the field. Next to the trail is a small pond, with egrets and mallards in it.

Belle is obsessed with birds. We took a bird-watching picture book from the San Francisco Public Library a few weeks ago, and Belle knew exactly what the birds were.

She points to the ducks. "That's a mama mallard," she says.

"Is it?" I say.

"See how she goes everywhere with the ducklings?" she adds.

I watch for a moment. Belle's right. Mostly the smaller ducks follow her, but if the ducklings take off in a different direction, she goes, too. "That's so nice," I say.

We both watch the ducks for a minute, not saying anything.

"Alex," Belle says, looking up at me, "why doesn't Mom go places with us?"

It's a great question. Our mom isn't working today. She works most Saturdays, but it used to be that when she had time off, she would spend it with us.

But she's been spending a lot of time with Xander lately—actually, doing stuff *for* him. She runs a lot of his errands, makes him food, and has started to drive even more of his shifts for UrbanGrub. He lets her use his car for that, but not for anything else (like driving me to a soccer game).

But none of that will mean much to Belle, so I just say, "I don't know, Belly Boo. She has to work a lot, and it's hard." Then I add something true. "But I'd rather be here with *you* than anyone."

She puts her arms around my waist and leans her head into me. "Me too," she says. We stand like that for a little while longer, watching the ducks swim and the egrets fish, and feeling the warm sun on our backs.

I feel content and relaxed when it's time to meet my team for warm-ups. I don't want to let anything Coach says bother me. I tell myself I might sit on the bench for the whole game, or that Coach might find a new way to criticize me, but that it won't matter.

None of that happens, though.

During warm-ups, Coach isn't *nice,* exactly, but he isn't mean, either. When the other coach comes over to introduce himself, Coach actually smiles and shakes the guy's hand. He's civil to the ref, too. Of course, the ref looks like one of the grumpy-old-man refs to me.

And then Coach gives us the starting lineup. My jaw practically hits the ground when he says my name. This will be my first time starting for Select, and I'm so excited to be in the game from the opening whistle instead of watching from the bench. We'll be playing a formation with two center strikers—Apple and me. Apple looks annoyed, but I don't care. We've never been on the field at the same time before, and suddenly I'm inspired to make it *work*. A plan pops into my head.

I learned during my first-ever soccer game that setting up teammates to score goals makes them happy. Now I'm going to do that for Apple.

Apple hasn't scored once this season, and I think behind all her smirking and eye-rolling, she's losing some of her confidence. That can happen to anyone, and it stinks. She's a good player, and if she plays well, it will help our team—in this game, in postseason tournaments, and if we make it to Nationals. I'm feeling so good after my time with Belle earlier, and I'm so happy to be starting, I think I can try to forget about how she treats me—at least during the game—and focus on supporting my teammate.

When the game starts, it's obvious that Apple isn't interested in doing the same for me. Or any of her other teammates, really. But especially me. It doesn't matter how many times I get open—she will not pass to me. Even when I'm right next to her in front of an open goal and she's being bombarded by two defenders, she won't send the ball my way.

She wants to be the one to score.

Fine.

The next time one of their defenders gets control of the ball, I crank my speed up and swoop in to steal it. The defender never sees me coming. She's back on her heels and I get around her easily. All I have to do to score is shoot it past the goalie.

But I don't.

I know Apple is sprinting toward the goal, and if I dish it off to her, she'll basically have a 100 percent chance of scoring. And as the goalie approaches me, I flick the ball to my left, to Apple. Apple stays calm and connects perfectly, with a low, hard shot to the corner.

We're up 1–0. And Apple has her first goal of the season.

I don't bother trying to high-five her or fist-bump her. I just say "Great shot" and run back to our half of the field to wait for the other team's kickoff.

"Nice pass," Apple mumbles.

At least, I think that's what she says. Whatever it is, it isn't loud. But it also isn't sarcastic.

We end up winning 3–0 that day. It's the first game in years when I don't score a goal. But I snag three assists, and Apple has a hat trick.

If she realizes how hard I worked to get her the ball, she doesn't say anything. But she definitely likes the attention she's getting from all of us on the team.

Everyone tells her what a great game she had. It must make her feel generous, because she does something I never expected.

I almost fall over when she pats me on the back and says, "Good game, Alex."

In front of our whole team.

I'm pretty sure a few of the girls sigh with relief when they hear that. Everyone has been able to feel the tension Apple has directed at me all season long. And the last thing we need on our team is extra tension. We get enough of it from Coach.

But what stuns me more than anything is the thing that happens next.

Coach *smiles* at us.

"Well done, Superior," he says. "The team you just played won the State Cup last year, and you shut them out."

It's as if every girl on the team grows an inch when he says that. "Apple, Alex, good work up front," he adds.

That's it, but it gives me a glowing-inside feeling. Which is unexpected, given who said those nice words. But yeah, praise feels good.

Apple smiles at me.

I think she's glowing inside, too.

Apple's dad comes over, with a huge grin on his face, to congratulate her. He doesn't do that after games if she doesn't score. She lights up when he praises her. When he sees me, he says, "Tough game for you. Good thing Apple showed up to play."

I let out a short, sarcastic laugh before I realize he isn't kidding. Okay. Was he even watching the game?

I try to tell myself that it doesn't matter what the Select parents think of me, but it still stings when they treat me badly. "Yeah," I say, rolling my eyes—although he's back to staring at his phone, so he doesn't notice. "Good thing."

At least my teammates—maybe even Apple now—are on my side.

As Belle and I walk the mile to the Caltrain stop, and as we stand waiting for the bus, I can't keep the smile off my face. It feels *good* to be part of a team, if that team likes and respects you. It seems like all of mine finally does. It doesn't feel quite like my old team—not yet—but it's getting there.

And that feels amazing.

19

AGAIN

COACH KEEPS UP THE POSITIVE VIBES FOR about one week after our shutout in San Mateo. We win 3–1 the next weekend, against a team that's very strong, but not quite as good as the San Mateo team.

Coach doesn't like it. After the game, he doesn't say much. But at our next practice, Coach is mad. Even though we only have one game left in the regular league season, plus a tournament, and we have won every game.

Which, Liv tells me, has never happened before.

But apparently it isn't good enough.

"That game was ridiculous," Coach says when we gather at the start of practice. "They outran you and beat you to every ball. You think you can play like that and make it to Nationals?"

He pauses, and I wonder if he will ever mention that we actually did win.

Nope. He's just doing his dramatic-effect-pausing thing.

"There will be extra sprints today," he says in a low voice. "Now get going with your warm-up."

It's like we had a week of sunshine, but the rain just came back. Or more like a hurricane.

This is not what I need today, of all days. Last night was a tough one in our neighborhood, and I barely slept.

At the end of practice, as promised, there are extra sprints. A lot more than usual.

"Again!" Coach says. We all drag ourselves back to the goal line, which we just crossed at a full sprint. No one says a word—we're all breathing too hard. Liv may be a keeper, but she is still one of the best runners on our team, and it looks like even she is in pain. My own legs are burning, and my lungs are on fire.

"Are you okay?" I ask her. She closes her eyes for a second, then nods. I pat her on the back to let her know I'm with her.

"Alex, get on the line," Coach says.

"I'm just checking on my teammate, Coach," I call. Because that's what a good teammate does, even though I know I'll probably pay for it later. Coach glares at me, muttering something under his breath.

We're running ladder sprints, from the goal line to the top of the penalty box and back, then to a marker halfway between the goal box and midfield and back, then all the way to midfield and back. As fast as we can. I've lost count of how many repetitions we've already done. When we finish the next one, several girls are doubled over in pain.

We always end practice with sprints. Coach reminds us that if we want to win every single game and every single tournament, we have to be able to "run the other team into the ground." But we've never done this many in a row. It's getting ridiculous. Maybe even a little dangerous.

Coach blows his whistle, and we all take off from the goal line yet again. I'm not the first to reach the top of the penalty box, but I'm second or third, I think. As I turn to run back toward the goal line, I keep my head down and push harder, ignoring Coach when he says, "Alex! You're dragging! You're not even trying."

I am trying, actually. I always try. And I'm usually the fastest.

But today, I'm exhausted.

Last night, someone was shot on the street outside our apartment around eleven p.m. Like, really shot, with a real gun. There were loud popping noises that woke up Belle and me. And my mom wasn't home—I'm pretty sure she was with Xander. Anyway, it's not like my mom could have done much to stop what was happening outside. But it was scary to be home without her.

It's happened before on our block, people getting shot. Belle and I watched through the window until the scene cleared. Then we tried to go back to sleep, but I heard Belle tossing and turning and sniffling in the bunk below me. I went down to snuggle with her, and I didn't sleep much after that.

So I've been pretty wiped out all day. I had a hard time concentrating at school. I even fell asleep while I was riding the bus to practice.

I think about explaining why I'm so tired. But, well, I'm too tired.

As we finish our millionth sprint of the day, I'm the first one to cross the goal line. I feel a little nauseous, but I know my teammates are hurting, too, so I turn right around to cheer for them as they finish. Zoe, who is the strongest player on our team, has to sit down because her legs are shaking. She puts her head in her hands, and her hair, which is woven into dozens of tight, tiny braids, falls in front of her face, almost like a shelter. I hope it protects her from Coach's anger.

But he doesn't yell at her. I look up and realize a bunch of parents, including Zoe's dad, and nannies are waiting across the field, watching. Practice was supposed to end a few minutes ago, so they probably got out of their big SUVs to see what the holdup is. Coach must see them, too, because he says, "Okay, that's enough for today. We're away in San Rafael on Saturday. Last game before State Cup. Be there one hour early to warm up."

I feel light-headed at the thought of it. Yet again, I have to figure out how to get to the game. I can do it, but at the moment, the idea of it is more than I can handle.

I just want to sleep.

I start walking with the other girls to pick up my backpack so I can head for the bus stop and get home to make dinner for Belle. That's when I hear Coach.

"Get back here, Alex. You could use a few more sprints. And then you can help me carry the gear to my car. You'll get the next bus."

I knew there would be payback for helping Liv and speaking up to Coach.

I never have a parent waiting for me, so Coach knows he can keep me after practice if he wants to. I'm trying to think of an excuse when I hear Liv call out, "Coach? Alex can't stay. She's getting a ride with us today."

Coach narrows his eyes at me, but he doesn't say anything.

"Sorry, Coach," I call as I jog toward Liv. Then I wish I could take it back. I don't have anything to apologize for, and I'm not sorry at all. Furious is more like it.

When I catch Liv, I say, "Did my mom set up a ride for today or something? I didn't know . . ." It seems impossible that she would have done that, or that she has any idea who anyone on my team is, let alone anyone's parent. She just doesn't have the energy for that.

"Nope," Liv says. "But he . . . well . . . We've all done enough sprints."

We're almost at her car, and her mom is smiling at us through her open window. Liv's dad could be a yeller at games, but her mom is one of the nice parents.

"Hey, Mom," Liv says, "can we give Alex a ride home?"

"Oh, that's okay," I say, knowing it's out of their way, because Liv's house is far from my neighborhood. Plus, I don't really want them to see where I live. "I can grab the bus—"

"Of course we can give you a ride, Alex!" Liv's mom says. "Hop in, girls."

Okay, a ride in their cushy car does sound nicer than a long bus ride. And who knows when I'll get this offer again. I'm too tired to argue, and I don't really want to.

"Thanks, Mrs. Thomas," I say. Then I look at Liv. "Thank you," I say to her, too.

I pause for a second. I really want to talk about Coach and the way he treats us. Get it out into the open. I know Liv sees it, too. But I glance at her mom, who seems so perfect and happy and has been so generous to give me a ride, and I'm not sure I should bring it up in front of her.

So I keep it to myself. But I look back at Liv, who gives me a sympathetic smile. It's good to know someone else is paying attention.

20

THE LADYBUG

WITH JUST A FEW MINUTES TO GO IN THE LAST game of our regular fall season, we are up 6–0. I have three goals and three assists. We are going to finish the regular season undefeated. We have already qualified for the fall State Cup, and our chances of qualifying for Nationals after the spring season are great. I may despise Coach, but I love (most of) my teammates, and I'm not going to let him get in the way of what we're all working so hard for.

As all these thoughts are running through my head, I see it.

A ladybug.

A lot of people think of ladybugs as lucky. I know I do, especially since they remind me of Evie.

Halfway through my first microsoccer season, everyone on my team had scored at least one goal—except for my teammate Evie. Evie wasn't usually part of the cluster of kids around the ball. She kind of wandered around on her own. Sometimes she picked flowers. And if she did, somehow, get anywhere near the ball, she froze.

While we were in the middle of our fifth game of that season, I remember checking in with her. She was squatting down in a far corner of the field and looking at something on the ground. I wondered if she was picking flowers again.

I ran over to her. "What are you looking at?"

She pointed to the tip of a blade of grass. "Ladybug," she whispered.

"Oh yeah," I said. "I see it. It's pretty."

From behind me, I could hear the other team getting ready to kick off.

"Come on! Let's go play," I said.

Evie shook her head. "Someone might step on it," she whispered, sounding sad. "We have to rescue it."

She had a point. "Okay," I said. The other team kicked off, and our teammates were calling for us. I looked back to Evie. "Do you want to pick it up and put it over there?" I pointed to a patch of taller grass, a little way off the field.

Evie nodded. I scooped the ladybug into my hand.

"Gentle!" Evie said. She came with me, and I let the ladybug crawl off my hand and onto a safe blade of grass.

Evie stood there watching the ladybug, but I grabbed her hand and said, "Come on!" and she ran with me back to the field. Where the other team was scoring a goal.

But Evie was beaming with pride. And so was I. Some things are more important than scoring goals.

I know exactly how Coach will react if I rescue this ladybug now, and I don't care. I can't leave this ladybug here to be stepped on.

As quickly as I can, I bend over to scoop it up, then run over to the edge of the field closest to a small garden and put it down on a plant.

"Alex!" Coach yells. "What are you doing?! Get back out there!"

Mission complete, I run back onto the field.

Unlike the time Evie and I performed a ladybug rescue, the other team does not score. Nothing bad happens.

Still, the next time the ball goes out of play, Coach subs me out.

I run over to the bench, and I can't stop smiling.

"*What* were you doing?" he splutters. There's actual foam at the corners of his mouth, and his face is bright red.

"Rescuing a ladybug," I say calmly as I sit on the bench.

Coach looks like his head might explode. "If you ever pull something like that again, you are off the team," he says, towering over me.

Now I feel like *my* head might explode. Does he want me to apologize or something? Because I'm not going to do it.

"Coach, we're winning six to nothing. I scored three goals. I have three assists. I left the field for five seconds to save a ladybug," I say. "I don't think you want me off the team."

He opens his mouth but doesn't say anything. His eyes narrow and he looks confused, actually. He wasn't expecting me to respond like that, and I'm pretty sure he can't come up with anything to say. I look toward the field, ready to pay attention to the game and my team-mates. He walks away, muttering words I won't repeat.

But I don't care. The moment feels like a victory. For our team. For the ladybug.

And for me.

21

WHY WE PLAY

IF YOU DON'T LIVE IN CALIFORNIA, YOU MIGHT assume that the weather here is perfect all the time. Sunny, warm, beach weather. That's how it is in some parts of California, I guess. It's not like that in San Francisco, though—at least not most of the time. Here it can be really foggy, and the afternoons get pretty windy. July and August are usually cold and gray. And in late summer and fall, we sometimes have to stay inside because of smoke from wildfires in Napa or Tahoe or somewhere else nearby.

But most years, in the fall, we get at least a few perfect days. The kind of days people think of when they think of California weather.

And that's exactly what we have one Friday afternoon

in early November, when Coach happens to be away at a tournament with his thirteen-and-under boys' team—the other Select team with a good chance to go to Nationals in the spring. Our regular fall season is over, but we have a few more tournaments to play, including one in the East Bay this weekend. And if Coach has to choose between coaching us and coaching the boys, he always goes with the boys.

Which is great.

Especially if Coach Rafa fills in for him, which he's doing this weekend. Rafa is the most fun of all the Select coaches. He's actually nice to us. And respectful.

I mean, he works us hard. I'm always wiped out by the end of one of Rafa's practices. But when you aren't worried that you're going to mess up and get in trouble, it feels less like work.

And it turns out we play better when we aren't nervous all the time.

That day we do a few drills, then play 2v2 games—Rafa sets it up like a tournament and calls it the 2v2 World Cup. Then we scrimmage. And I swear we play better than ever.

With about forty-five minutes to go in practice, Rafa calls us over for a quick chat.

"Are we doing sprints now?" Sera asks, a touch of

dread in her voice. No one likes sprints much, but she hates them. A few girls groan when she asks this. If we start sprints now, we're going to be doing them for a long time.

But Rafa says, "Sprints? Nah. You have a tournament tomorrow. But here's what we're going to do to end practice."

I brace myself. The end of practice is never easy.

"See over there?" Rafa points to the trees at the western edge of our practice field. The Great Highway and Ocean Beach are on the other side of the trees.

We all look.

Light from the setting late-afternoon sun is glowing pale yellow through the spaces between the trees. We can hear waves crashing. It's magical.

"That light is awesome," he says. "And it will be even better on the beach. Come on. We're going to jog over there—no sprinting—and end with some beach soccer."

My jaw drops. Beach soccer? We've been practicing a minute away from Ocean Beach for months, and we've never played beach soccer.

But then I get worried. My backpack from school is here, with my bus pass and my phone and my school shoes. I can't just leave it here.

"But, Coach Rafa," I say, "what about our stuff?"

If I had asked Coach that, he would have yelled at me. But Rafa just smiles.

"No worries," he says. "Coach Lindsay on the next field is my buddy. She coaches for Girls Together. I'll ask her to keep an eye on our bags, 'kay?"

"Okay!" I say.

Rafa runs over to Lindsay, who gives him a thumbs-up. "Have fun on the beach, girls!" she calls to us. And so we head to the beach.

We take off our cleats at the edge of the sand and play in socks and shin guards. We're only there playing for about twenty-five minutes before we have to jog back to the field to make sure we aren't late for pickup time. But it's twenty-five minutes of pure fun. We fall down a lot, and everyone is laughing—I don't think I've ever seen this team laugh together—and the ocean is sparkling. No one keeps score. And I absolutely love it.

I think everyone on my team agrees. As we walk back to our practice field, Rafa takes one last look at the ocean. "That was fun, right?" he says, smiling. Then his voice gets serious. "Just remember that having fun is why we play."

That weekend in the tournament—well, maybe it's a coincidence. Maybe we would have won anyway. Maybe it has nothing to do with that fun beach soccer practice.

But we play more like a team than we ever have before. And we crush it in the tournament.

Some of that energy stays with our team through the fall State Cup tournament, which our team wins easily. It may help—okay, it definitely helps—that Coach is at State Cup with his thirteen-and-under boys and Coach Rafa fills in again. Either way, we come home as champs.

22

FUTSAL

AFTER WE WIN THE STATE CUP, I ASSUME I'LL be getting a break from Select, at least until spring practices start.

But it turns out there's an optional futsal season that runs from January to March. We get an email about it right after State Cup. Futsal is indoor soccer that you play on a hard court. We sometimes played futsal at the rec center on rainy days, and it's really fun. The ball goes fast. You can score a lot of goals. I always loved it. When I think about playing futsal with Coach, I just want to take a nap.

I wonder if anything is really optional when it comes to Select. So I text Liv and Amelia to ask if they're going to sign up to play futsal. Amelia responds right away.

> Um, yeah. Not really optional.

Liv responds later that day.

> You have to sign up for futsal if you want to play in spring.

So, there isn't going to be a break. Do I want to play in spring? Well, yeah. Of course I want to play soccer.

But do I want to play for Select?

To be honest . . . I don't know. I like my teammates. We are really good, and we have a great shot at making Nationals. Just the thought of that fills me with adrenaline. But all that comes with Coach.

Still, I'm obviously not going to let Coach keep me from soccer. I love the sport, and my teammates, too much. So I register for the futsal league.

And almost immediately get an email with a bill for three hundred dollars.

Which we can't afford to pay.

I wonder if any of the other players on the team even

think about how much three hundred dollars is when your family doesn't have much money.

It's not nothing. It's *a lot*.

I go back and look at all the information Coach sent when I initially signed with the team. It says that my regular-season fees and uniform costs are covered. It doesn't mention "optional" things like futsal.

So now I'm going to have to tell Coach we can't pay for futsal, so I won't be able to play in the league. I'll train with Jayda at the rec center instead.

When I think of playing with Jayda instead of Coach, it feels like I just put down a heavy backpack. I feel light, and I start getting excited.

I decide email is the easiest way to tell him, so I send a quick note saying how much I wish I could play (*ha*) but that my family just cannot pay the three-hundred-dollar fee.

Just when I think that's the end of it, my phone rings. It's Coach. I think about ignoring it but decide to deal with him.

I press accept. "Hello, Coach," I say.

He doesn't bother saying hello.

"So. You *really* can't figure out a way to come up with three hundred dollars for winter training?" he asks.

"After we gave you thousands of dollars in handouts this fall? And considering all the handouts you'll get this spring?"

My mouth opens, but at first no words come out. I never asked for any handouts. Having me play for his team for free was *his* idea. Is he really giving me a hard time about not having money?

"No, Coach," I say firmly. "We can't."

He pauses, then says, "You don't train through the winter, you don't play in the spring."

"I'll be training through the winter either way, Coach," I say. "I never stop playing soccer. But we can't pay three hundred dollars for the futsal league. So," I add, "if that means I can't play for Select in the spring, well . . ."

He's quiet. He waits. I don't finish the sentence. I'm not going to say anything else until he does.

Coach sighs, sounding annoyed. "Okay, what *can* you pay?" he asks.

I'm tempted to say, *Nothing. I can pay nothing. So I'm not playing,* but I wonder if I've pushed it enough, and that would be the end of my time with Select.

But just as I imagine leaving Select before spring, the idea of Nationals flashes through my head, and I pause. I hear myself say, "Maybe . . . a hundred?"

Which is way too much. I don't have one hundred dollars. I'm sure my mom doesn't have a spare hundred.

Coach sighs again.

"Fine," he says. "I'll change it to one hundred dollars as a favor. But, Alex," he adds, "you'd better play like you deserve this."

He hangs up.

"I don't even want to play for you!" I say angrily into the phone. But of course he can't hear.

I'm breathing hard, and my hand is shaking as I put my phone down. I close my eyes and feel my hands clench into fists. I take a deep breath and try to relax so my heart will stop pounding.

If we make it to Nationals, it'll be worth it. It has to be.

And now I have to figure out where I'm going to get one hundred dollars.

My mom is not happy when I tell her about the money. (I don't mention that it was supposed to be three hundred dollars.) The fact that it's for Select makes it a little better, but she shakes her head and says, "I just don't have that much extra. Can't you get this for free, like everything else with that team?"

"It's not free, Mom. Believe me, I'm paying for it."

"What?" she asks, confused. "What do you mean?"

"He treats me differently, and not in a good way. He expects more from me and respects me less than anyone else on the team. I'm pretty sure that's because I'm playing for 'free,'" I explain.

She sighs. "Oh, Alexa. I guess when you get something for free, you have to work a little harder for it."

"I don't mind working hard," I say. "I work *very* hard. But he doesn't respect me. I know when someone disrespects me. It's something we should all be aware of," I say, looking pointedly at her. She either doesn't notice or doesn't have the energy to respond to that.

She just says, "I can try to work even more Urban-Grub shifts for Xander." She rubs her eyes and yawns. And I am reminded that regardless of the things she does that I don't agree with, she is trying. I can't ask her to work more than she already does.

"It's okay, Mom," I say. "I'll figure something out."

So I put up signs around our building saying I'm available to help with babysitting, dog-walking, and cleaning for low rates. I don't know how people feel about hiring a twelve-year-old, but they like my prices, so I get a ton of calls and texts. I also tell Mrs. Lopez in our building that Belle and I will keep watching her toddler whenever we can. She has a little baby, too, and she seems so grateful for any help. I tell her I feel bad about charging her, but she laughs and says it's okay, because we are the most affordable babysitters she's ever met.

For the next couple of weeks, between school and soccer and hanging out with Belle and all my paying jobs (Belle almost always comes with me to do them), I feel like I'm trying to swim in really deep water and only barely keeping my head up. But soon I've earned $122.

I give one hundred dollars to my mom, and she pays the futsal bill with her credit card.

I take Belle out for ice cream with five dollars.

I keep the other seventeen dollars. I have to start saving just in case there's something else for soccer that I need to pay for. We keep helping Mrs. Lopez with her toddler, too, and she keeps paying us. Little by little, my seventeen dollars grows.

And then futsal season starts. We get the official schedule about a week before our first game. And when I see where we will be playing, I actually laugh out loud. When we got the sign-up emails, there were alerts that the locations were changing, and I wondered how far I would have to go to get to them. Now I know.

I won't have to go far at all.

Almost all of the games are in *my* neighborhood, or very close by. For once, I will be the one who doesn't have to worry about how to get to a game. Because I can just walk.

I wonder how the girls on my team—well, their parents, actually—are going to feel about playing in a gym in Chinatown and the Tenderloin. I've been to the gyms where we are playing, and I know they are great spaces. But I have a feeling the parents will find plenty of reasons to complain, because they aren't fancy, and the streets are narrow and crowded.

The futsal games turn out to be more fun than I expect. Several players, including Apple, miss a bunch of games because of "prior commitments." Meaning their families would rather leave the city to go to their ski houses than hang out in a gym downtown. They paid for the season, of course, but it turns out Coach doesn't care so much about kids *playing* futsal. He just wants them to pay the fee. Anyway, the kids who do show up get to play the whole time.

Better yet, Coach's boys' team happens to have most games scheduled around the same time as our games.

Which means Coach goes with them and misses all but one of our games. For the other games, Coach Rafa fills in for him.

Which means we just play.

And we have a great time.

23

GETTING SERIOUS

BY MARCH I KNOW BETTER THAN TO EXPECT A break between the winter season and the spring season. I figure our twice-a-week practices will continue without even the tiniest pause right through to our last game.

But then Coach makes an announcement at one of our sessions. It's chilly and dark at the end of practice. It's one of those San Francisco days when the outside temperature doesn't tell the whole story. The wind, especially near the ocean, cuts right through the sweatshirt I'm wearing. I sweated while playing, but when we stop moving, I start shivering quickly.

I'm not the only one who's freezing. We all gather in a group around Coach, and as I look around I see that everyone is shivering. Ellie's teeth are actually chattering.

"Okay, everyone. See you here tomorrow," Coach says.

"Tomorrow?" a few people ask.

"We're getting serious now. It's all on the line this season," Coach says. "You want to make it to Nationals, right? To win Nationals?"

No one speaks.

"So we'll be practicing four afternoons per week," Coach continues. "And this season, it's every girl for herself. You don't help me win, you don't play. I want you out there on the field fighting against your teammates to be the very best player on the field, every time."

Wait. He didn't say "fighting for your teammates." He actually said "fighting *against* your teammates."

What is *wrong* with him? I shouldn't be shocked by anything he says at this point, but I still am.

"Everyone understand?" Coach asks.

"Yes, Coach," a few girls mumble. I don't say anything.

No one looks happy. But I guess his plan works somehow.

When the spring season starts, we keep winning and winning. Getting closer and closer to Nationals, even if we're all having less and less fun.

24

HE NEVER EVEN PLAYED

GOING INTO OUR LAST GAME OF THE SPRING season, we are undefeated in the top division of the NorCal premier league. We haven't even tied a game, and we are definitely going to qualify for postseason play. But Coach expects us to win every game, and he's still encouraging us to play to beat each other as much as we play to beat our opponents. At the end of one practice, he threatens something new.

"I need to see one hundred and ten percent effort at every practice and every game, and if I don't . . ." He pauses and looks around, giving me an extra hard look, then continues. ". . . I can and will cut players before the postseason."

I force myself to keep a straight face. He doesn't scare

me. He's not going to cut me. Coach and I actually want the same things: to make Nationals. To win Nationals. And to do that, he needs me. We both want our team to be the best we can.

And in the last game of the season, we are.

Our opponent is the toughest we've played yet. F.C. Mountain View. They won the State Cup last spring. We've never played them.

The first half is a battle. We come close to scoring, but their defense is strong and their goalie is the tallest girl I've ever seen on the field. She saves everything. She's amazing. It's 0–0 going into the second half.

But then Apple gets the ball around midfield, and I see an opening. "Send it!" I call to her, and take off running, ready to slip between two of their defenders as soon as the ball gets there. She knows what I want to do, and instead of trying to beat a bunch of players on her own, she connects with the ball and lofts it up and over their back line.

I know exactly where it's going.

I get to the ball, and my first touch puts it out of reach of their defense, but not too close to their goalie, who is charging out toward the ball. With the goalie a little out of the net, I take one more touch, then chip the ball up and over her head. It comes to rest in the back of the net. And we are up 1–0.

I race over to Apple, ready to give her all the credit. "Great ball!" I shout, then pat her on the back as we jog to our side of the field. "Great shot," she replies, and I feel warm inside.

The battle continues, and neither team is able to score again for most of the rest of the second half. Liv is on fire, stopping every shot they send her way. We are still up 1–0 with less than a minute to play.

Then a ball brushes Amelia's hand in the goal box. It's accidental and unintentional and has zero impact on the play. Still, the ref blows his whistle and gives the other team a penalty kick.

The other team is excited, and some of the players are already high-fiving each other. I shake my head a little. You never celebrate a goal *before* it happens.

Yes, a PK is going to give them a great chance to score. But they don't know who they're facing in the goal.

Liv stands on the goal line, arms stretched to the side, on her toes. I can tell that every muscle in her body is tensed and ready to fly. She stares hard at the player from the other team. I smile as I watch her. I would not want to be the one getting stared at like that.

The player makes the mistake of looking directly at Liv and sees the fire coming out of her eyes. Suddenly the player looks nervous, and nervous is not a good way to feel when you're about to take a PK. The best penalty kickers are the ones who stay totally calm. Who don't try to do anything fancy. Who approach the ball and send a confident shot into a far corner of the goal.

This player doesn't stay calm. She shoots, and Liv can tell exactly where it's going. Low and to the left, but not far enough to the left. Liv makes an easy dive and gets there before the ball does.

Save. I stand still for a moment, a feeling of joy and pride for Liv spreading through me.

Then we all swarm around Liv, giving high fives and hugs, and the ref blows the whistle. Game over, and Liv is definitely the MVP.

Not that Coach ever names MVPs. But wow, she was awesome throughout the game, and saving the PK was other level.

I'm not sure what I expect Coach to say about Liv's amazing save. I know it won't be much, but I think he'll at least mention it. He doesn't.

He interrupts our celebration, and he looks angry.

"One-nothing. You keep saying you're going to win Nationals, and you only beat this team one-nothing?"

My joy disappears. First of all, *he's* the one who keeps saying we're going to win Nationals. But he isn't even close to done ranting.

"And you almost tied. They never should have been in our end. Total defensive letdown. And you," he says, pointing at Liv. "You almost let in at least three. Plan on some extra training if you don't want to be on the bench next game."

We all stand there with our mouths open. Coach has players he picks on, sure. I know that better than anyone. But he has never done it to Liv.

"Coach," I say, "Liv was amazing."

"Yeah," Amelia chimes in. "She is the reason we won that game."

I'm not sure he even hears us. He just stomps away.

We all turn to Liv, who is staring after Coach, a look in her eyes even more intense than the one she had right before the PK. I speak first.

"Liv, that's so wrong. You were amazing today."

"Amazing," Ellie repeats.

The rest of the players start talking at once, telling Liv what an incredible game she played.

"I know that," she says, and the entire team quiets down. "He wants to bench me in the next game? Fine."

She strides off the field toward our gear, finds her

backpack, and starts shoving her stuff into it. I'm pretty sure I know how she feels. I follow her.

"Liv, are you okay?" I ask.

She looks up, and I half expect to see tears in her eyes. But nope. She looks calm and powerful. Coach doesn't get to Liv the way he gets to the rest of us.

"I'm *fine*," she says. She looks toward the parking lot, where Coach is getting into his car. "He calls other coaches idiots? *He*," she says, "is an idiot."

She stands up and slings her backpack over one shoulder. "You know," she adds, "I didn't even want to play on this team. And I'm not just saying that because I'm mad right now. I tried out for four great teams and I made all of them. I wanted to play for Girls Together, but my dad thinks Select is the best club to play for if you want to play in college. Because that's what Coach told him." She rolls her eyes. "He also couldn't remember my name for like the first three months I played for him. He even introduced me to another coach as 'the sister of Matt Thomas, who plays soccer for Stanford.' I hate when people define *me* by what my brother does, you know?"

"Yeah," I say, nodding. I wouldn't have thought of that. When she says it, though, it makes so much sense. "I doubt he'd ever introduce a boy on his team as the brother of some great girl soccer player."

Liv tilts her head to the side. "You think?" she says sarcastically.

Then she sighs, and the expression on her face gets more serious.

"Nope, he wouldn't," she says. "And by the way, it's definitely *not* okay that he does stuff like that to us."

"Neither is the mean stuff," I say. "But it's not just that he's mean. He's mean *and* he's sexist."

"That is correct," she says.

"And not just with us," I say as the picture continues to sharpen in my head. I think about the way he treats female coaches and refs—which is very different from how he treats male coaches and refs. "He's awful to coaches and refs who are women, too."

Amelia's voice comes from behind me. "Yup. We were talking about the definition of misogyny in my social studies class at school. I'm pretty sure there's a picture of Coach next to it in the dictionary," she says, hands on her hips.

"But," she adds, "when I tried to tell my parents that, they told me I was overreacting. That I need to forget about all that and concentrate on soccer."

"My dad said pretty much the same thing," Liv says. "At least my mom paid attention. She wants me to switch teams. My dad keeps saying Select is the 'best route to playing in college.'" Liv makes air quotes with her fingers. "But if Select makes me hate soccer, why would I want to play in college?"

That's a good point. I think about what Jayda said, about not forgetting how much I love soccer.

Liv shakes her head.

"You know he never even *played* soccer, right?" Liv says very casually. So casually, I figure I must have misheard her.

"What?" I ask. "Who never played soccer?"

"Coach. He never played soccer," she says again.

"Wait," I say. "The guy who tells us all the time how different women coaches don't know anything about soccer? *He* never played soccer?"

"Nope," Liv says. "Never."

It's as if bells start clanging inside my head as my mind starts racing—and a plan starts forming.

"Maybe," I say slowly, "we'd be better off with a coach who did."

Amelia raises her eyebrows. Liv smirks. They both start nodding. And that's the moment when I start dreaming about what it would be like to be on this team with a different coach.

25

WE'RE IN

AFTER OUR SPRING SEASON, WE WIN THE State Cup, which is a qualifier tournament for the US Youth Soccer Far West Regional Championships. So obviously we qualify, and then we win Regionals, too.

Which means that for the very first time, our team is going to the US Youth Soccer National Championships.

And Coach wants us to win. He wants that very, very bad, because it would be the best advertising ever for his club. I also want to win, but for different reasons.

Coach wants to win because then he can say a Select team is a national champion, and even more people will want to try out for his club. Players from all over the city—and towns all around here, sometimes an hour or more away—come every spring to four rounds of tryouts, to try to earn the right to pay thousands of dollars every year to be on a Select team. And sure, some of the teams—like ours—are very good. Not all of them are, though, but they are all expensive.

I don't pay to be on the team, so obviously I'm just here to help him win.

Which makes me feel torn. Because I *want* to help my team win.

But I don't want to help Coach.

26

PIZZA PARTY

ABOUT A MONTH BEFORE NATIONALS, COACH IS pushing us harder than ever, and he decides we should practice every day. He calls it Nationals Training Camp. It starts at the end of June, when all of us are out of school for the summer, so it could have been like any other soccer camp. Except he runs it from eight a.m. to six p.m.—longer than any day camp. And there are no fun games or treats or prizes or anything campy like that. Just drills, scrimmages, and then sprinting.

When he first tells us about it, my first thought is, *I can't go.* It's summer, and Belle isn't in school. Our mom works every shift she gets. And she's driving Xander's UrbanGrub route for him more and more often. She says she does it for extra money, which we definitely need. And then she brags that she gets to keep half of whatever she earns—which is ridiculous, because she's doing all the work. When I try to explain that to her, she gets mad at me and tells me I don't get it.

She's right. I don't.

Anyway, Belle can go to the rec center during the day, but during the summer it closes at six. If my practice doesn't get out till six, I won't get there to pick her up till 6:40 at the earliest. And these days, with our mom running every time Xander calls, I don't feel like I can count on her to remember to pick up Belle every night.

But my mom swears she'll do it. "Promise!" she chirps. "If Coach Austin wants you there, you should be there," she says.

No matter what I tell her about the things Coach has said to me, she tells me to ignore it and keep playing for him. I know she wants to help me. I know she thinks this is my ticket to college. But I wish she would really listen. Once she even tells me to try apologizing.

"For *what*?" I ask.

"I don't know, but could you just say you're sorry?"

When she says that, I feel like a deflated balloon. "You want me to apologize for being a girl? For being myself? For scoring twenty-one goals this season? Mom," I say quietly, "if someone treats you badly, it's not because *you* did something wrong. And there are a lot of different ways to hurt someone."

Tears well up in her eyes. "How did you get to be so wise?" she says. "See, this is why we need to make sure you can go to college."

So of course I go to Nationals Training Camp.

The days are long and cold during that first week of camp. We are having a foggy week, and summer in San Francisco can be freezing when it's foggy. Especially near the ocean. I get home at almost seven most nights. And I have to leave before seven each morning to catch the bus to camp. My mom is only late to pick up Belle one night that week, on Tuesday, but Jayda is there, and she stays with Belle and keeps calling my mom until she reaches her.

By Friday, the whole team is wiped out, and camp is running really late. It's already after seven when Coach calls us over.

"I know you all think this has been a long week," he says.

We look at the ground, at each other, anywhere but at

him. I'm tired. We're all exhausted. It's a pretty stupid training strategy, if he wants us to go into Nationals with any energy.

"Yes, I heard a few complaints," he says, and then actually smiles. It's one of those smiles that doesn't get all the way to his eyes, but it's still a smile. "So tonight, before you go, we are having a pizza party."

This is about the opposite of what I expect him to say. I glance around at the other players, who look as shocked as I feel. Just then, a delivery person walks onto the field, carrying a stack of pizza boxes. "Where should I put them?" she calls.

Coach looks annoyed at the interruption, but he gestures at her to put them down anywhere. He does not say thank you, I notice. She puts them on the ground and leaves. Coach continues, "I let your parents know we'd be staying a little late, so don't worry about that."

This is all so weird. Pizza sounds amazing, and I'm starving after the long day of soccer—there wasn't much food at home to pack for my lunch. But this seems too good to be true.

"Well?" Coach says. "Go ahead. Have some pizza."

We look at each other again, then slowly walk over to the pizza.

Oh, wow. It smells delicious.

We hesitate. Then Liv opens one of the boxes, grabs a slice, and takes a bite. Slowly, the rest of us start taking slices of pizza, too.

Then, surprisingly, Coach wanders to the other side of the field, looking at his phone, not paying attention to us. Everyone grabs more slices, and we're all talking and laughing. There's plenty of pizza. I eat three slices. I'm thinking about having a fourth when I hear Coach's voice.

"How's the pizza? Anyone want more?" he asks.

No one does, now that he's right there. People finish chewing and don't take another bite.

"Done? All right, then," Coach says. Then his voice turns colder than the fog. "Go line up for sprints."

What?

We literally just finished scarfing down pizza. And he wants us to run sprints?

Oh. It *was* too good to be true. The pizza wasn't a reward.

It was punishment for complaining, I suppose. Or being tired and hungry. I don't know, but I think he's trying to show us what happens if we don't behave exactly the way he wants us to.

It's beyond unacceptable. I'm furious. And I'm not the only one.

Before we line up, Liv stands and starts walking away.

"What are you doing?" Coach calls. "Get on the line now, *Olivia*."

When Liv hears her full name, she turns, looks at Coach, and says, "No."

The rest of us freeze.

"What did you say?" Coach asks in a low voice, pointing at Liv.

"I said no," Liv says, through clenched teeth.

"Get on the line, or you're off the team," Coach says, taking a step toward her.

"No," Liv says. Then she shrugs her shoulders. "I guess I'm off the team."

And she just . . . walks away. It's fantastic.

"Get back here!" Coach yells after her.

Liv keeps walking.

"You quit this team, and I'll make sure you never play soccer again!" Coach yells, and I realize that he's starting to sound desperate.

Liv never turns around. I'm nervous, but I know what I have to do next.

I see through the fog that her mom's car is already there, waiting. So are many of the other parents' cars. I wish I had someone here for me. It would make what I'm about to do much easier.

Amelia and I look at each other, and I can see the determination in her face. Then we look at the rest of our teammates. Everyone is looking at each other with wide eyes, and there's a buzzing energy in the air. Like something big is about to happen. I can tell Amelia feels it, too. We need to choose right now between supporting Coach and supporting our teammate. I know what I'm going to do. I think I know what Amelia is going to do. I have no idea what anyone else will do.

Coach recovers his composure and yells, "Everyone else, on the line. Now!"

I respond loudly. "No."

And I walk off the field, grab my backpack, and follow Liv toward the parking lot.

27

LET'S GET OUT OF HERE

MY HEART IS POUNDING AS I WALK AWAY FROM the field, but I know—*know*—I've done the right thing.

And I'm not the only one.

Unlike Liv, I do look back. And I see Amelia, Zoe, Ellie, and Sera walking away from Coach. The rest of my teammates—even Apple and Veronica—follow us. Amelia catches up to me and puts her arm around my shoulders for a quick hug. "I'll talk to you tomorrow," she says. She glances over her shoulder at Coach, who is gaping at us. I expected him to look angry, and maybe he does a little, but mostly he looks shocked. "Let's get out of here. Now."

The other girls look scared, but also proud. I know

how they feel. Several of them pat me on the back before they jog to their cars.

"Thanks," Sera says to me. "I don't know if I would have done that if you and Liv didn't go first. Can we give you a ride to the bus stop?"

"Yes," I say, grateful that I can get out of there quickly, and that I won't have to walk alone through the park at night, and that I have a team to support me right now. "Thank you."

28

WHERE ARE YOU?

SERA AND HER MOM WAIT WITH ME UNTIL I climb onto the bus. As I do, I realize my legs are trembling a little after everything that just happened, and I sink into the closest seat. There's a film of cold sweat on my neck and back. I try to breathe slowly. I take a deep breath in and let out a long exhale. Then I reach into my backpack to grab my phone so I can text my mom and let her know I'm on my way.

There's a long chain of texts from her, plus seven missed calls. The first text came at 6:15.

> Where are you?

Then another at 6:17:

Home soon? I'm driving UrbanGrub for Xander tonight, so come straight home for Belle. See you later.

That's weird, because she knew I wouldn't be home by then. Even if Coach let us out right at six—as if he'd ever do that—I wouldn't be home till 6:40.

Okay. I know I'm running late. Really late. But my mom told me—she *promised*—that she would not forget to pick up Belle like she did on Tuesday, and that she would be home with her tonight. But did she leave, thinking I'd be home right away?

Has Belle been at home, alone, waiting for me, for all this time? I hate thinking of her by herself in our apartment, probably scared. I can't call her, because she doesn't have a phone. All I can do is hope the bus moves quickly.

And all I can think about is wanting Belle to feel safe. I wonder if my mom will keep driving if she doesn't hear from me. If Xander tells her to, she probably will.

I text my mom back.

I won't be home for 35 min. Can you go home till then?

I watch my phone, waiting for my mom to read my message, and for the little dots to appear to show that my mom is responding.

She must be dropping off food, because she isn't reading it. I wait for five minutes as the bus moves along Fulton, where there isn't much traffic at this time on a foggy summer Friday night. My teammates were talking earlier about going to their houses in Sonoma and Carmel and Tahoe for the weekend. Everyone else in the city is probably already there, too.

During other weekends, I'd feel jealous about that. But now I just want to go home, hug Belle, and go to sleep.

I check my phone again. More than ten minutes have passed since I texted my mom, and she still hasn't read my message. It just says "delivered." Why is she ignoring me?

I think about Belle all alone, and I'm starting to get frantic.

The bus has been stopped at an intersection for a while now, and we aren't moving. I stand up to see if I can figure out what's going on. A huge line of bicyclists is streaming through the intersection, blocking traffic.

It's Critical Mass. Normally I think Critical Mass— a huge monthly group bike ride around the city that basically stops traffic wherever it goes—is the coolest thing ever. It's a group of things that are less powerful (bikes) trying to stop something that's more powerful (cars, trucks, and buses). They work together and make it happen.

I just wish they weren't making it happen right here, right now.

We wait. And wait. I feel like I'm about to jump out of my skin, and I'm checking my phone every two seconds. Two older women in the seat in front of me keep looking back at me with worried looks on their faces. I don't think they speak much English, but they try to comfort me anyway.

"It be okay," one of them says. "It be okay."

I hope she's right. I close my eyes and try to breathe slowly, thoughts of Belle being alone and my team and what Coach did tonight jumbling together in my brain. Just then the bus lurches forward and I stumble into the seat in front of me. We're moving again.

I sit down and alternate between checking my phone and closing my eyes for the rest of the ride.

It's almost nine o'clock when we get to my stop, and it's totally dark. I race off the bus, calling good night to the older women and the bus driver over my shoulder. I have my keys out as I run to the front door of our apartment. I know I'm hurrying too much but I can't seem to slow down, and at first I keep fumbling with the key and can't get the door unlocked.

Finally I get the door open and race up the stairs, my legs somehow managing to move after all they've done for me today. Before I put the key into the lock in our apartment door, I call, "Belle, it's me. It's Alex." I don't want to scare her. Then I unlock and open the door.

The living room is dark, but I hear a sniffling sound coming from somewhere inside. I turn on a light. "Belle?" I say quietly.

I hear a loud sniff, and then Belle says, "Alex?"

Her voice is coming from a corner of the room, behind the couch where our dad used to sit when he watched TV. I find her there, sitting on the floor, her knees pulled tightly to her chest and tear stains on her cheeks.

"Oh, Belly Boo," I say, and get down on the floor next to her. I put my arms around her, and she leans against me. I can feel her relax as she does.

"Where were you?" she asks. "Mom said you'd be home soon, and she went to work. That was a really long time ago."

"I'm so sorry, Belly Boo. I was at practice. Coach kept

us even later than usual. Have you been sitting here since Mom left?"

Belle nods. "I thought you were coming right home, so I waited here. I wanted to be hiding in case . . ."

She doesn't finish the thought, but I can imagine some of the scenarios that might have run through her head. When you're seven and home alone in an apartment in a neighborhood where bad things sometimes happen, any scary thing seems possible.

"Well, I'm home now. And I'm not going anywhere. Let's get ready for bed, okay?"

"Okay," Belle says. "Will you sleep with me?"

"Yeah," I say, and squeeze her to me. "Of course I will."

We go into our room and I help Belle find her favorite pajamas. While she's brushing her teeth, I text my mom.

I'm home. Belle was here alone for almost THREE HOURS. What were you thinking?!?!?

This time, she does respond.

You just got home? Oh no. I messed up. I'm sorry. Coming home now.

I don't even want her home now. I can't believe she did this to Belle. I toss my phone onto the counter in the kitchen. I don't want to text her again while I'm still mad.

Instead, I take a quick shower, brush my teeth, put on sweats, and snuggle up with Belle in her bunk. I read her one of the Fancy Nancy books that we got from the library. She thinks they're funny, which is exactly what she needs right now. She's asleep before I'm even halfway through, and I finish reading it to myself—I need something silly, too.

As I close the book, angry voices start coming from the street below. I realize our window is open a crack, and I get up to close it. I look down and see my mom and Xander, standing next to his car. I've only met him once before, and as I watch him yell at my mom, leaning over her as he jabs his finger into the air, I feel nauseous.

"This is it? That's all you made tonight? You gotta get back out there," Xander says to her.

"I worked as long as I could, but I'm going home to my girls now," she says.

Xander says some swear words, and my mom starts to apologize with her head down. But then she stops.

"You know what?" she says, lifting her head and suddenly standing up a little straighter. "I'm not sorry. I told you I couldn't work at all tonight, and I shouldn't have. I'm done. And it's time for you to go."

"What did you just say?" Xander asks, anger in his voice.

"I said it's time for you to go," my mom repeats, with enough strength to show she isn't kidding.

Xander calls my mother a nasty name and raises his hand, and I gasp. For a moment, I wonder if he's going to hit her. But then he gets into his car and speeds away, tires squealing.

My mom shakes her head as she watches him drive down the block, then comes inside.

I'm still mad at her, but I've never seen her stand up to anyone like that. I'm shocked, and I can't help feeling proud of her for standing up to that guy.

When she walks into our apartment, I tiptoe out of our room. "Hi, Mom," I say.

"Alexa, I'm so sorry," she says, but I cut her off before she says more.

"Just . . . please, Mom . . . just don't leave Belle home alone like that again."

She nods. "I won't," she says. "I mean it."

Then her phone rings.

I wonder if it's Xander, calling to apologize or something. And I wonder if my mom will fall for it.

But it isn't Xander.

She wanders out of the room to take the call. She says, "Oh, *hello*, Coach Austin. It's nice to hear from you."

I feel my insides turn hot. My anger, which subsided while I was comforting Belle, swells back up again. Why is he calling now? To cut me from the team?

I have no idea what Coach is saying, but I hear my mom laugh. It makes my stomach queasy. Partly because she no longer seems to feel sorry about what she did, and partly because she's talking to Coach. Who I never, ever want to see again.

I had hope for her when my mom told Xander to get lost. But she has not figured out the deal with Coach, obviously.

A few minutes later, she comes into the room, smiling. "I know it's been a rough night," she says, "but I have some good news. Coach Austin is starting a new team in the fall. An eight team, or something like that." She claps her hands together, delighted.

Okay, *what*? After everything that happened tonight, he calls to talk about a soccer team for little kids? Was he trying to figure out how much my mom knows about what happened? Is he worried I'm going to quit?

But instead of saying any of that, my mom smiles. "And he wants Belle to come play for him."

29
THAT'S IT

IT FEELS LIKE MY STOMACH DROPS TO THE
floor when my mom mentions the idea of Belle playing for Coach. It didn't even occur to me that this was
something I'd have to worry about, and it's too much. I
can't take it. And I don't want to talk about it.

I don't respond. I just turn and walk into my room.

I climb back in with Belle. But as Belle sleeps, my
mind is racing. I won't risk having Belle left alone like
that again. I can't practice every day until six o'clock anymore, and if Coach has a problem with that—which he
will—I will quit the team and find a new one. And I'll
go to Nationals with them. Select is not the only club
that can make it to Nationals.

It hits me that I am the leading scorer on my team.

I have more assists than any other player, too. The team has had its first two undefeated seasons since I joined. Select needs me more than I need them.

I start to get angry. Angrier than I've ever been in my life. Angry at Xander for taking advantage of my mom. Angry at my dad for the way he treated her, and us, and then just disappeared from our lives. Angry at my mom for not standing up to them.

But most of all, I'm angry at Coach, and the way he sucks all the joy out of playing soccer. I think of the toxic, competitive vibe he creates on our team. Of all the mean comments and the disrespect he shows to me, to my teammates, and to every female coach and referee he encounters. The way Coach treats my team and punishes us, just for being girls.

And I'm angry because he came close to doing what Jayda warned me about when I first told her I was playing for Select: he almost made me forget how much I love soccer.

And now he wants my sister to come play for his new U8 team?

No way is that happening.

30

CALL IT WHAT IT IS

WHEN BELLE GETS UP IN THE MORNING, I GIVE her breakfast, then take her with me to the rec center. Our mom is still sleeping, and I leave her a note so she'll know where we are. But there's no way I'm letting Belle out of my sight today.

I'm relieved to see that Jayda is there, kicking a ball in the courtyard with a few kids around Belle's age. When we get closer, Belle realizes that two of them are girls from her team. "Vivi! Maya!" she shouts. She starts to run over to them, but then stops and returns to me. "Come with me," she says. "Please?"

So we run over together.

"Alex and Belle! Hi, girls," Jayda says. "How are you?"

"We're . . . uh . . . we're okay," I say. "Can I talk to you for a second?"

"Of course," Jayda says. "What's up?"

"Um . . . could we talk . . ." I look at the little kids. "Could we talk by ourselves?"

A worried look passes over Jayda's face. She motions for me to follow her to the edge of the courtyard. I turn to Belle before I go with Jayda. "I'll be watching you," I promise.

"Will I be able to see you the whole time?" she asks.

"If you look, I'll be there," I say. "But you might want to watch the ball, too," I add, smiling.

"Okay!" Belle says, and I go with Jayda.

I don't know how much time I have before Belle comes to find me again, so I start talking right away. The words come out quickly, like a rushing river tumbling over rocks. I tell her about the way Coach has treated me since the moment I was a minute late to warm up for my first Select game, about the comments he makes to me and other players, and "running like girls." The way he insults and threatens me, the way he disrespects me and other players on my team, the ways he treats us differently from his boys' team, the way he disrespects female coaches and referees. The way some of the parents treat me. And finally, I tell her what Coach did last night, and how Belle was left alone, and that Coach wants Belle to come play for him.

Jayda listens to every word. And then she waits, making sure I've had a chance to say everything I want to say. Most adults don't do that, when kids are talking.

"Oh my god," Jayda breathes. "Thanks for sharing all of this with me." She pauses. "First of all, are you and Belle okay?"

"We're okay," I say. "We were both scared, and I'm not leaving Belle alone again. Like, ever. But we're okay."

"Alex, you can always call me if you need help with Belle. I'm here for you guys."

"Thanks, Jayda," I say.

"And now I need you to listen to me. About the stuff with Coach."

I feel so much calmer after unloading all of that. Calm enough to listen.

"There's nothing wrong with a coach being tough and expecting a lot from players. But that's not what this is. He insults you. He scares you. He compromises your safety. That isn't tough coaching. That's abuse."

I'm nodding along with her until the last thing she says, about abuse. "But, Jayda, I don't know if it's abuse. It's not like he hits us or hurts us or anything," I say.

"There are different kinds of abuse," Jayda says quietly.

"And we have to call this what it is. It's verbal abuse. Emotional abuse. Psychological abuse. Those things are very, very real. And very, very hurtful, even if they don't leave you with physical scars."

I nod slowly. "But why? Why does he do it?"

Jayda shakes her head sadly, and shrugs. "Because he can? I don't know. I don't know him. He's in a position of power, and the ones he abuses most are the ones he feels like he has the most power over. He doesn't think you can do anything about it."

This makes sense, too. Because what could *I* do about it?

"He has been hurting you. He has been hurting other players. It's time to put a stop to it," she continues. "When you realize there's a fire, you have to do what you can to put it out. Before it gets bigger."

"But how do I do that? I can quit the team, but no one will care," I say.

Jayda smiles at me. "From what I've heard, your team will care very much if you quit," she says. "But you're right. Just quitting probably won't do it.

"You have to talk about it. You have to get other people to talk about it. This kind of abuse keeps going when it's in the shadows, where most people can't see. You need to shine a spotlight on it."

I'm not sure how to do that.

But I think it's necessary.

"I don't want to make everyone quit the team, though. I don't even want to quit, really. But I don't want to play for Coach again."

"So . . . ," Jayda says. "What *do* you want?"

That isn't a question I'm asked very often. It feels nice to be asked. And I know exactly what I want.

"I want to play at Nationals. With my team. But *without* Coach."

"Okay," Jayda says. "So how are you going to do that?"

I sigh. "I don't know. It's impossible."

"Don't say it's impossible," Jayda says. "Think about it before you give up."

"Okay." I pause and think. "We need a different coach," I say. "We need an incredible coach. One who knows way more about soccer than Coach does. One who played in college, because that's what all these parents seem to care about."

Jayda tilts her head to the side and smiles. "Like me?" she says.

My eyes get wide.

Back when I played with Jayda, there wasn't much talk about playing soccer in college. I never asked about it, and she never mentioned it. But when I think about it,

I realize she does have some incredible moves. She's the one who taught me about juggling, and who showed me that it was possible to juggle hundreds of times. And she definitely knows *a lot* about soccer.

"You?" I say, and a warm feeling spreads over me. A feeling of hope.

"Well, I played in college. Division One, at USF. I was a four-year starter and an All-American. If that's what the parents care about," she says. "And yeah, I know way more about soccer than your coach—excuse me, your former coach—does."

"That's funny," I say. "You know, Coach thinks *you* don't know what you're doing." I roll my eyes.

She stares at me. "Someone doesn't know what he's doing," she says. "But that someone isn't me."

31

WE CAN DO THIS

THE IDEA OF PLAYING WITH MY TEAM IN NA-
tionals with Jayda as our coach has me more excited
about soccer than I've been since . . . well, since before I
left my rec center team to play with Select.

And I realize that, just maybe, it could actually work.
By some stroke of luck, Nationals are being held in Sacramento this year, which is only a two-hour drive away.
Most of the girls on my team complained when they first
heard where the tournament was, because they wanted
to fly across the country. It didn't occur to them that the
cost of a plane ticket would make it impossible for some
of us.

Like me.

Plus, I'm certainly not going to travel to any tournament without Belle. And buying two plane tickets? Doubly impossible.

I'm not sure, but I get the feeling Jayda doesn't have a lot of extra money, either. I could never have asked her to buy a plane ticket—and it's not like Select was going to pay for her to take over one of their teams.

Anyway, the fact that the tournament is in Sacramento is incredibly lucky. The money I've been earning from helping Mrs. Lopez in my building might be enough to cover bus tickets for all three of us. Four, if my mom wants to come.

I try to think through as many details as possible to make sure we can pull this off. I call the US Youth Soccer main office to explain that our team has qualified for Nationals, but we want to go with a different coach. They say as long as we have at least twelve of the players from the team roster that got us this far, we can play. No guest players. Our roster has sixteen total. That means four people can say no, and my team can still play at Nationals. But it's going to take work.

I make my first phone call to one of my teammates. Well, technically I text first.

Liv, can you talk? ASAP?

My phone rings almost immediately.

"What's up?" Liv asks.

"Want to go to Nationals?" I ask.

"Alex," she says. "I'm *not* playing for Coach. I don't care if it's Nationals. I wouldn't care if it was the World Cup."

"But what if you didn't have to play for Coach?" I say.

She pauses. "What do you mean?"

There's a hint of excitement in her voice.

"What if our team goes to Nationals with a different coach?" I say.

"What coach?" she asks.

"Jayda," I say.

"Your Jayda? The famous Jayda from the rec center?" Liv asks.

"Yup," I say. "That Jayda, but how does everyone know who she is?" I ask, remembering that Amelia has heard of her, too.

"She's a legend," Liv says. "Every club in San Francisco wants her to coach for them, but she won't leave the rec center."

"How did I not realize that?" I say. "You know, I once heard Coach say she doesn't know what she's doing. But she does. She's legit."

"Oh, I know. She's definitely legit. But . . . we

can't . . . Can we even do that? Play with another coach?" she asks.

"We can," I say. "We can do this. If we have at least twelve players from our spring roster."

Liv doesn't hesitate.

"Who should I call first?"

It's simpler than I thought it would be. We start by calling Amelia, Ellie, and Sera. They are all in, with no hesitation.

Then we start reaching out to other families. When Liv and I talk to our teammates and their parents and lay out in detail all the ways in which Coach abuses his players, most of them acknowledge that it's the truth.

They just needed someone to say it.

In the end, only Apple decides to stick with Coach, instead of with us, her teammates. I'm not even sure it was actually her decision. If it were up to her, she probably would come with us. Liv tells us that Apple's dad refused to let her leave Select and play "for some idiot coach who doesn't know what she's doing."

Hmmm. I wonder where he got that line about Jayda.

Instead, Apple is left with no team. No trip to Nationals.

And, as it turns out, no Coach.

It all takes a few weeks, but when the news gets out about our team leaving Select as a group—and *why* we're leaving—lots of players start coming forward with their own stories of his abuse. Some of it is even worse than what we experienced. Coach is banned from ever coaching youth soccer again, and Select is disbanded.

In the best twist, the other teams and coaches all go to a different club. And that club is Girls Together.

Even the boys' teams.

"We don't practice gender discrimination here," the founder of Girls Together explains in an interview that she does after the story about Coach breaks. It's big news, at least in the California soccer world. "Everyone is welcome."

But that all comes later.

The afternoon before we are supposed to leave for the tournament, I'm at the club, practicing juggling with Belle and working on my own juggling record. I'm having trouble getting more than one hundred, which is weird for me. But I can't quite get into the zone—that headspace where everything seems to slow down and I get totally relaxed and feel like I could juggle forever. I'm thinking too much about the tournament. What if we get crushed? And after all we did to get here, what if everyone blames me for it?

I'm finally getting into a bit of a juggling groove—seventy-six, seventy-seven, seventy-eight—when Jayda comes into the courtyard. If I had been truly in the zone, I wouldn't have noticed. But I look up, and when I see the expression on her face, I let the ball drop.

She's furious.

"What's going on?" I ask, nervous. Instinctively I look at Belle. She's still right there, and she's fine. But I don't think I'll ever not check to make sure she's okay, ever again.

"I just got a call from George Preston," Jayda says. The way she pronounces his name makes it sound like she's talking about rotting garbage.

"Who?" I ask.

"A dad of one of the players from your Select team. Apple's dad," she explains. "He says if we try to play in Nationals using the Select club name or wearing Select uniforms, he will sue me and every family of every player on our team."

"Can he do that?" I ask.

"I have no idea," she says. "But I don't think we can risk it."

I groan. "What are we going to do? Go to Nationals but not be a club team? Will people think we're just a bunch of rec players instead of a real team from a competitive travel league?"

"Does it matter?" Jayda asks. "Whether people think you're rec players or comp players or whatever—I am so sick of all that," she says, rolling her eyes. "It's why I keep coaching the rec center team, even though clubs try all the time to get me to coach one of their 'comp' teams. How about this: You're just a team of players. A great team. Of great players. And it doesn't matter whether it's rec or comp or Nationals. You just play. Just. Play."

"Okay, fine," I say. "But we need something to wear while we 'just play.'"

"Well," says Jayda, smirking, "I might be able to get us some rec center shirts. They're old, and a little beat-up, but I think they'll do the trick."

I think about the way Coach and my teammates looked at me when I showed up to my first Select practice in one of those old rec center shirts. I told Jayda about it, and she obviously remembers, too. I feel a smile spreading across my face.

"Perfect," I say. "Perfect."

I go back to my ball for one more round of juggling. I flick it up with my toe and find a rhythm easily. The world falls away. I'm in the zone. It's just the ball and me.

One hundred.

Two hundred.

Five hundred.

Jayda is watching, quietly, and I know she's rooting for me. But she does nothing to distract me as I go all the way up to one thousand and then keep going. I am in the totally relaxed zone I need to be in to keep going. Suddenly I'm passing sixteen hundred. I've never gotten this high before. I've smashed my old record. I make it to 1,821 juggles before the ball hits the ground.

I look up at Jayda and smile. She is grinning at me. My arms and legs are tingling, and I feel something I haven't felt in almost a year.

Pure soccer joy.

32

LET'S DO THIS!

WHEN THE REF BLOWS HER WHISTLE TO START our first round game at Nationals, I'm nervous. Not nervous like I was with Coach, but nervous because I want so badly for our team to do well. To show that I didn't make a huge mistake when I suggested this. To prove we belong here.

But it wasn't a mistake. We do belong here.

We win 3–0 against a really good team from Massachusetts. I feel bad that they traveled so far only to lose in the first round.

But not too bad.

After the game, we give the other team a cheer. (And our pregame cheer was *not* the signature Select cheer, but a simple "Play hard! Have fun!") We eat snacks. We talk. We laugh. We feel like a team.

Our second game is closer. We are playing against the top-seeded team in our age group. The team everyone expects to win. They are a fancy club team—or at least they look like it, based on their uniforms and warm-up gear and their five coaches in coordinating uniforms—and they score on us quickly to go up 1–0.

They are really, really good. They're fast and skilled, and they can make spectacular passes, although a few of them seem to want to score without help. We tighten up our defense and mark their best players, and the score is still 1–0 at halftime.

When we gather around Jayda, she is glowing with pride. I knew she would be, but I think the other girls on my team are still getting used to that.

"Girls, this may be the best soccer game I have ever watched in my life. And I've watched a lot of good soccer," she says. "You are playing brilliantly."

"But we're losing," Amelia points out.

"True," Jayda says. "By one goal, to the top-ranked team in the country. But okay. You want to win. You stepped up the defense just like you needed to in the first half, and you need to keep that going. But you also need to figure out how to beat them on offense. They are too good for anyone to do it alone," she continues. "You're going to have to do some of the best passing you've ever done. Quick, one-touch passing. Look for the holes in their defense and pass right through them. When you're off the ball, look for the runs you can be making to give your teammates someone to pass it to. Keep the ball moving so quickly that they don't know what hit them. As a team. Got it?"

"Got it," we say.

And we do, from the opening whistle of the half. We play with our heads up, constantly looking to pass to each other, or move to space where we can get a pass. We run hard and pass precisely. Ten minutes into the half, I get the ball from Amelia and look up to see Ellie streaking toward the goal. I send the ball through a hole in the defense, just like Jayda said I should, and Ellie gets there at exactly the right time. She doesn't fiddle around with it, trying to set up the perfect shot. She just fires hard, shocking everyone, and sends the ball into the upper left corner of the net. Score: 1–1.

Each half of our soccer games is thirty-five minutes long, and for the next twenty-four minutes, no one scores. But it's the best soccer I've ever played. Apparently I'm not the only one who thinks the soccer is good, because a pretty big crowd has gathered on the sidelines to watch us play—although I'm so focused on the game that I barely notice.

I hear Jayda call, "Less than a minute, girls! Let's do this!" I've never worked so hard in a game, and I should be wiped out. But I feel a surge of adrenaline as I realize how amazing it is that we are here, at Nationals, with Jayda coaching us.

The ball is deep in our end, but Amelia is there to clear it. She passes it out of the middle to Sera, and I see my chance. I call to Sera once, and she sees me. She sends a perfect long ball across the field and over the heads of our opponents' defenders. With every ounce of energy I have left, I sprint toward where I know the ball is going. Their defenders are fast, but somehow I know I can beat them . . . and I do. I control it and immediately take a shot with my left. The ball slides past the other team's goalie, low and hard to the corner.

2–1. Before I have a chance to process what just happened, the ref blows her whistle three times. The game is over. And we are heading to the semifinals.

Every girl on our team jumps about a mile into the air, and then we come together in the middle of the field for a huge group hug. Cheers erupt from the sidelines, too, and not just from the families of our players, but from all the teams watching. Including, I notice, a boys' team. The boys, in fact, are cheering loudest of all.

After the game, one of the boys from that team runs up to me. "Hey, you're Alex, right? I'm Jack. Great game," he says. "The passing was amazing. We're gonna try to pass like that in our next game. So . . . thanks," he adds, then smiles and jogs back to join his teammates.

I smile, too. I'm not sure they can pass quite as well as we just did, but I'm rooting for them.

33

THE BEST

GAME THREE IS THE SEMIFINALS. IT'S OUR toughest game yet, which makes sense. I have chances to score, but I just can't get the ball in the net. Neither can my teammates, no matter how hard we work together. The score is 0–0 after the end of regulation time. I find myself wishing Apple had come with us. We're good together, up front.

We go through two overtime periods and there's still no score.

Finally, we go to penalty kicks. Five each.

I shoot first. I know I can do it, because I've practiced this a million times. I stay calm and knock one in with my left foot, at a perfect angle to the lower right corner.

Belle cheers, and I wave to her. It's always great to have

Belle at my games, but hearing her sweet voice at this tournament means more to me than it ever has before. She's on the bench with our subs, where she can be Jayda's assistant coach, and where Jayda can keep an eye on her.

Our mom couldn't come. She wanted to, but she needed to take on another work shift, since she's not earning extra money by driving Xander's UrbanGrub shifts anymore.

It's okay. I have Belle. I have Jayda. I have my teammates. And before we left, my mom pulled me into a hug and whispered, "Good luck, Alex. I'm proud of you for being so strong." It was the first time she called me Alex with no prompting and complimented me on something other than my outfit or how I looked. I hugged her back, hard. And I know I wouldn't be here without her.

Our opponents shoot next. Liv stands ready on the goal line, staring down the shooter with her don't-mess-with-me look. It works. The shot sails just over the crossbar.

Ellie shoots next for us. She scores, too, in the upper left corner. Our opponent misses again.

We're up 2–0.

Then Sera shoots. Our opponents' goalie tips it wide.

Then Liv saves one.

We're still up 2–0; our opponents missed their first

three shots. All we have to do is make one more shot to win.

"Liv should shoot," I call to Jayda.

"What?" Liv asks. "Why?"

"Because," I say, and walk over to her. "Because you were the first one of us who really stood up to Coach. Because you're the best keeper in the world. And we wouldn't be winning without you. We wouldn't even be here without you. You should finish this."

Liv grins. "Coach would never let me do this."

"I know," I say. "But Coach isn't here."

The players from the other team look confused when Liv steps up to shoot. But there's no confusion about what happens next. Without hesitating, Liv fires a perfect shot into the upper left corner.

And our team, which has been through so much and is now standing on the field at Nationals in our fraying rec center shirts, is heading to the national championship game.

I would like to end this story by saying we win Nationals.

But we don't.

We come close, but we lose 2–1 in that final game. We play our hearts out, though. And Kiyomi's parents come with her and a few other players from my old rec team to cheer for us. Even though I hate losing, there's a lot of love waiting for me as I come off the field.

So maybe we aren't the best team in the country, but we are definitely one of the best. And who knows? On another day, against a different team, we might have won. Maybe we will win next year.

But it doesn't really matter.

Because we are a team. A real team. We support each other and respect each other. We have fun.

And that *is* the best.

When we gather around Jayda after the game, she looks at us with so much pride that she's practically shining. "You girls are amazing," she says. "I love watching you play. So what do you think—should this rec center team give it another go in the fall?"

"Yes!" we all shout.

And although I'm sad this season is over, I'm excited to play again.

Luckily, I don't have to wait long. For the rest of the summer, Jayda holds an optional—truly optional—weekly practice at Kimbell, a great turf field that's half-way between my neighborhood and the neighborhood where most of my teammates live. On the evening of our first practice, Belle and I arrive early with Jayda, to help her set up. I wonder how many of my teammates will come, even though this team has no fancy club affiliation or professional-looking uniforms.

I shouldn't have worried.

Every single one of my teammates shows up, with huge smiles on their faces. Everyone is chatting and laughing as we warm up, including Jayda. We have a juggling session, and Jayda gives everyone tips for getting better at it. We do a bunch of fun, active drills. We scrimmage. We don't do sprints, although Jayda says we will sometimes. That's okay. Sprinting can help make you faster and stronger, but it shouldn't be a punishment.

It's the best practice I can remember having since before I joined this team.

And I realize that I can't wait for the fall season to start with this team.

Can't. Wait.

I feel like I'm five and a half again.

AUTHOR'S NOTE

Approximately 70 percent of kids drop out of sports by age thirteen. And by age fourteen, girls drop out of sports at twice the rate boys do.

If you ever think about dropping out of sports entirely, I hope you'll reconsider. There are many reasons to play sports, and not only if—like Alex—you're hoping to play for a college team. Sports can give you an adrenaline rush in the healthiest possible way. They give you the chance to bond with teammates and form lifelong friendships. They inspire you to work hard and push yourself to get better. It's incredibly satisfying to practice hard—and then to see that work pay off during a game or race. And, oh yeah—sports are *fun*.

By the way, you don't need to pick one sport at an early age and devote your life to it. In fact, some of the best athletes in the world played lots of other sports when they were kids. I hope you'll try different sports and stick with the ones you like best.

But what if you have a coach who is making you miserable? One who is verbally or emotionally abusive, or abusive in some other way? To be clear, a coach who expects you to work hard and be respectful or who gives you honest feedback is not being abusive. Most coaches are not abusive.

But some are. This is a serious issue, and you should talk to a trusted adult immediately. Ask for help so you can get yourself into a better situation.

Also, a note to parents and caregivers: Please remember that the most important thing you can do to support your child in sports is just show up and pay attention. After the game, the best thing to say—the only thing you need to say—is this: "I love watching you play."

And to all young athletes: Whether you play a lot of sports, are trying a brand-new sport, or are dedicated to a specific sport, I hope you always remember how much you love to play.

RESOURCES

Women's Sports Foundation

womenssportsfoundation.org

Positive Coaching Alliance

positivecoach.org

Respect in Sport

respectgroupinc.com/respect-in-sport

Childhelp

childhelp.org

ACKNOWLEDGMENTS

Endless gratitude to Tricia Lin, the most thoughtful, compassionate, and insightful editor I could imagine. Thanks to Stacey Glick, agent extraordinaire. Thanks to the team at Random House Books for Young Readers: Caroline Abbey, Mallory Loehr, Jade Rector, Megan Shortt, Barbara Bakowski, Katharine Wienecke, Rebecca Vitkus, Shameiza Ally, John Adamo, and Dominique Cimina. Thanks to the amazing Grace Johnson and Jenni Johnson. Thanks to Alison Engel and to the Literary Masters fourth- and fifth-grade book clubs. Thanks to all the good, kind, supportive coaches out there, including Lindsay Kauffman of Girls Unite; the inimitable Tracy Capone; and Ashling Bryant, whose postseason poetry is absolutely epic. Thanks to the parents of Blitz FC for trusting me to coach your girls for ten seasons. And, as always, infinite gratitude and love to Ellie, Jack, and Vivi.